Solomon and the Queen of Sheba

Great Romances of the Bible Series

Rena Jones

Loper Publishing

Loper Publishing

ISBN: 978-1-969028-09-0

Printed in the USA

Contents

Chapter One

The Girl in the Shadows

The night palace breathed in incense and secrets.

Palm shadows latticed the flagstones; oil lamps burned along the colonnade. She crouched behind a screen of carved cedar, with ibexes and palms. Her knees tucked to her chest, her braid pinned high, she made herself small against the wood. The cedar was cool against her cheek. Through the filigree, she could see her father's hall of counsel: the gold-threaded canopies, the braziers where frankincense tears smoked pearly and sweet, the long, low tables laid with ivory tablets and reed pens. Men of the kingdom sat in a half-moon—merchants in linen with kohl-dark eyes, priests with clean-shaven crowns and lapis amulets, generals with sun-brown forearms and scars they did not hide. At the center, on a lion-footed chair, her father listened.

They did not know she listened too.

"Majesty," said the merchant with the ash-colored beard, "the incense road is bled dry. Raiders levy tolls or set fires. Our camels return thin as reeds. If we cannot move our resin north to the Nile and beyond, the temple lamps will grow dark."

A murmur. The priests bowed their heads over their rings and whispered among themselves. The general on the right shifted, the leather of his belt creaking. He wanted swords, she could tell it by the way his hand lifted to the hilt of nothing, even here.

Her brother lounged just behind their father, elbow on the arm of a chair not meant to be sat upon. The heir's signet—heavy, newly made—caught the lampfire whenever he gestured. He was handsome when he smiled, careless when he did not. Tonight, he did not.

"Speak plain, Haran," her father said. His voice was low, like a drum. "How many caravans lost, and where?"

"Two, Great Lion. At the wells of Kadar. The band that calls itself Moon's Claw demands a tenth of every load and a girl for their lord each season."

At that, the hall went still as a held breath. The priests' whispers died. Even the brazier hissed a little more softly. Her father's face did not change.

"Names," he said. "We deal in names, not shadows."

"None worth speaking," Haran said. "But—" He gestured, and a slave boy brought a basket forward. "A sample from the last shipment. Judge for yourself, Majesty."

The boy set the basket near the foot of the dais and uncovered it. Her father took a piece of resin between forefinger and thumb—a pale, translucent lump like a frozen tear—and lifted it to the light. A breath of the scent rose, clean and bright, pine and lemon and something that made the mouth water. It should have been perfect, she thought. And yet she was already leaning forward, eyes narrowing.

Not all the pieces gleamed evenly. Some were dull, chalked at the edges. One showed tiny black grit inside, as if a fly had drowned in it when it was soft. She pressed her palm to the cedar and felt its grain. Someone has adulterated this, she thought, and not the raiders—Haran, whose sandals drag like a man who lives in counting houses, not in desert wind.

Her father rolled the tear of resin between his fingers. "The road is dangerous," he said. "This is known. But this—" he lifted the piece, turning it so the light slid along the blemishes "—is not the road's doing." His eyes flicked across the hall, unhurried, resting on Haran only for a heartbeat. "Priest Zoher, what do you see?"

Zoher leaned forward, the lapis on his chest catching lamplight like a calm strip of river. "Some tears are pure," he said slowly. "Others are...clouded. They smoke too thick when burned."

"Confirmed by the last offering," another priest added softly. "The smoke did not rise straight. It hung heavy. A sign—"

"A sign," her brother cut in, with a glance at the priests that was half pleasure, half contempt, "that Haran's men scraped the trees at the wrong season or padded the baskets. Either way, the gods are not to blame."

A ripple of laughter, quickly swallowed. Her father did not rebuke him, but the air cooled a little. He set the resin back and gestured to a guard. "Bring a pan," he said. "We will burn a few."

The guard strode out and returned with a shallow copper dish and a brazier coal cupped in tongs. Her father dropped three tears into the pan and held it over the coal. Two bloomed into white smoke, thread-fine, and drifted straight as a prayer. The third smoldered and spat, sending a gray coil sideways that crawled along the table like a snake seeking a hole.

"Interesting," her father murmured.

Haran licked his lips. He had not expected a test. "The raiders—"

"The raiders do not mix chalk with the trees," her father said gently. "They only take."

The general's hand had drifted to his belt again. "Majesty. Give me fifty riders and leave to hang Moon's Claw from their own well."

"And where will you find them?" her father asked, still gentle. "They are night and dust. They are there and not there."

"Let me go," her brother said, sitting forward. "Not fifty. Twenty. Swifter. We will bait them at the wells and strike as they sleep."

He meant it; his blood had risen, his eyes were bright. The men in the hall breathed a little faster. Swords and punishment were the music they liked. The girl behind the screen pressed her lips together so she would not speak aloud.

The raiders were not the heart of the thing. Men who lived by stealing did not adulterate resin to shade a ledger. Haran is bleeding both sides, she thought, and if you cut off raiders and leave him, the smoke will still hang.

Her father's head lifted slightly. That tiny tilt, as when a lion catches a sound the gazelles have not heard, always made her throat ache with pride. He knew the room had shifted. He knew the place where the unseen thread ran.

In their private language—a language of knocks and scratches on wood learned when she had been barely taller than the arm of his chair—she tapped twice against the cedar: Wait. Look closer.

He did not turn. But his ring finger drummed the arm of the chair, once, twice. Go on.

"Haran," he said. "You brought the sample. Good. You will not mind if we use your balance."

"My—Majesty?"

"Your merchant's scale. I see it at your belt. Bring it."

Haran hesitated half a heartbeat, then unhooked the small bronze scale and brought it forward. Her father nodded to the guard. "Fetch water."

When the jar came, he gestured for Haran to hold the scale while the tears were weighed—pure against suspect, the little weights set with care. Then he asked for a second pan and poured water. "Drop the cloudy ones," he said.

They fell and fizzed, a faint dust unfurling. The clean tears did not, being resin to the heart. Haran swallowed. Her brother's mouth curled in satisfaction; the general looked ready to draw his absent sword and be done with it.

But her father did not strike. Not yet. He looked past Haran to the line of clerks. "Scribe," he said, and a thin man stepped forward, reed pen trembling slightly. "Bring the ledgers for the last three caravans through Kadar. The ones Haran company tallied, not the temple's—his house books."

A hush. Haran bowed, face smooth, but sweat had broken beside his ear.

"You mean to open a merchant's private accounts?" the priest Zoher murmured, wary. Power balanced between temple, throne, and market like a three-legged stool. Tip one leg and men fell.

"I mean to open a wound and clean it," her father said.

The ledgers came—thick boards bound with cord, smelling of dust and honey. The scribe turned the pages with careful fingers; numbers lined up like troops, tidy and brave. Her father read without moving his lips. He always read that way, letting the marks become speech inside his skull. When he looked up again, the night seemed to lean with him.

"General," he said mildly, "if you had a man in your ranks who stole a handful of grain from each soldier, what would you call him?"

The general was not a man of words, but he knew this answer. "Thief."

"And if, when you discovered him, he cried out that there were foxes in the chicken yard, would you chase the foxes or take the thief by the neck first?"

A slow smile creased the general's scar. "I would take the thief, Majesty."

Her father nodded, and the lion that lived in his voice put its paw on the room. "Haran son of Abir, your scales are false and your ink is crooked. You will repay double what you have taken to the temple and to the crown. Your house will be inspected by men who have no cause to love you. If your books are clean after, your name will be clean. If not, then may the desert forgive what the law will not."

Haran opened his mouth and closed it. He tried again. "You cannot—"

"I can," her father said softly. "You are not the first man to bring a basket to my table."

The priests said nothing. The general inclined his head, as if that were the end of it and he could go put the fear of the crown into Moon's Claw besides. Her brother was flushed with triumph he had not earned, and that made the pain sharp in her chest. He was bright and brave, and he moved always toward the shout. He did not love the quiet that made this possible.

The council moved on—wells to be guarded, decoys to set along the road (her father proposed them before the general could, and improved them besides: not one caravan, but three, staggered; the last heavy with water skins rather than gold), agreements to be inked with Nile traders who would take good resin for fair copper and grain. Each matter was a thread; her father laid them straight, smoothing tangles with the heel of his hand, until the cloth of the kingdom lay flat again.

When the men had gone and the lamps had been turned down and the braziers banked to a red glow like sleeping hearts, he said into the hush, "Daughter. Come."

She stepped from her screen and walked the length of the hall, the hem of her white linen whispering against her ankles. He had never called her by name in the hall. It warmed her and frightened her in the same breath.

"You should sleep," he said, but his eyes were amused.

"So should you," she said, and the answer made his mouth soften.

He took her hand, turned it palm up, and traced a line across it with his forefinger. "What did you see?"

"The resin," she said. "And Haran's sandals. The dust in the seam was not desert dust. It was chalk."

Her father's laugh was a small thing, but it traveled easily. "You see with more than your eyes."

"I hear with more than my ears," she said, a little boldly. "I hear whose voice grows thin at the end of a sentence when he lies. I hear where the fear is."

He did not chide her boldness. "And if you were seated where I am," he said, "what would you do about Moon's Claw?"

She had thought about it the entire night until the thought had become a shape with eyes. "Leave the wells dry," she said. "Seal them for a week. Let the raiders watch our caravans and find only thirst. Then open the wells again and send a caravan that looks full, but is full of guards who have been thirsty too long."

His finger stilled on her palm. "And when they take the bait?"

"Break them," she said simply. "Not to boast. To make the road safe, and because a well belongs to the people, not to a claw named after a moon."

He squeezed her hand and released it. "You are my daughter," he said, and for a moment the king fell away and there was only a man who had held her when she was slick with birth oil and wept into her hair. "Remember this: a king's first strength is patience. A second is good ears. The third is friends who tell him when his ink runs crooked."

"And the fourth?" she asked, smiling. This was their game. He liked to end with a riddle.

"The fourth is knowing when to be stone and when to be water," he said. "Stone for raiders. Water for fear. Water finds every crack, and in time even stones learn its name."

She tucked that into herself like a seed.

They walked the hall together, past the banked braziers and the lion-footed chair. The moon lay long on the floor like a spilled silk. At the door to the courtyard he paused, listening. Dawn was still a long climb away, but the city had begun to turn in its sleep—the clink of a mule in its stall, the distant cough of a man at a gate, a woman's laugh where it should not be.

"Some will say a woman cannot rule," he said, as if the thought had come on its own feet. "They will say it softly at first and then louder. They will say the gods do not bless it. They will say your hands are too small for the reins."

"My hands are mine," she said.

"They are," he agreed. "And they are not small."

He reached to the table near the door and picked up a small thing wrapped in linen. "A gift," he said. "Not for ornament." He unfolded the cloth. The amulet beneath was old, its gold rubbed thin where fingers had loved it. A lotus bloom, delicate as breath. Egyptian work. Her mother's people had brought it when she came to this country, a bride with Nile water still in her hair.

"Wear it at your throat," he said. "Remember that a river feeds more than one land."

She bowed her head and let him tie the cord. The metal warmed quickly against her skin.

"And now," he said lightly, "to bed with you, girl in the shadows."

She turned to go, then hesitated. "Father," she said without looking back. "If I were—if I were not in the shadows—would you still listen?"

He did not make it easy for her. He never had. "Make me," he said softly, "unable to do otherwise."

She went then, barefoot along the cool tiles, through a courtyard where a fig tree leaned over a pool and fish slept bright as coins. In her chamber she lay awake a long time listening to the palace breathe. When she slept at last she dreamed of a road that crossed deserts and seas, and of a voice far away that was not a voice but a rumor made of many mouths. A king whose judgments turned into proverbs. A temple that shone like a second sun.

But in the morning she woke to the sound of a pigeon on the sill and the smell of bread in the ovens and the knowledge that she would take her place behind the cedar screen again. She would learn the shape of every voice that sought to move her father's hand. She would mark which rings flashed when lies were told, and which eyes watered when justice fell.

She would make herself so keen that when the time came—whether they shouted for her or shouted against her—it would not matter at all.

Power, she had begun to learn, did not live only in the chair with the lion's feet. It lived here, in the shadows, where a girl could see.

Chapter Two

A Broken Scepter

The city awoke to mourning bells.

At first, the sound carried like a mistake, one heavy toll instead of the dawn drums. Then another, and another—slow, deliberate, echoing down every street until the dogs stopped barking and the market women froze with baskets in their arms.

In the women's courtyard, Makeda was already standing, hair unbound, long and loose, her sandals half-laced. She had not yet eaten the morning bread when the first cry went up from the gates: *The prince! The prince is fallen!*

Her breath turned to stone in her chest. She ran, skirts whispering like frightened wings, through the colonnades to the hall where her father sat enthroned.

He was there, face gray as the carved lions beneath him, hands gripping the arms of his chair until his knuckles showed pale. Before him lay her brother's armor, dented, splashed with the black crust of blood.

"He went to hunt lions," a captain said, voice broken like a reed in floodwater. "We warned him the gorge was treacherous, that raiders tracked the game. He laughed. He spurred his horse. He—" The man bowed his head, unable to go on.

Her brother. The boy who had teased her mercilessly when they played at chariot races in the courtyard. The one who had sneered gently when she whispered answers behind the cedar screen, telling her she was clever but that cleverness was not for queens. The one with sun in his hair and impatience in his eyes. Gone.

Her father dismissed the captain and the guards. He sat with the armor between them, staring as though he might command it to rise and bring his son back.

"Makeda," he said at last, and his voice was not the lion's drum of judgment now. It was a reed bent under storm. "My heir is dust."

She sank to her knees, laying her cheek against the cool iron breastplate. Tears blurred the world until it was only color and ache.

Later, when the kingdom's grief turned to murmurs, she heard them: *The gods are displeased. The line is broken. A woman cannot rule. We will need another prince from a rival house. Perhaps Egypt will give us one. Perhaps the generals will choose among themselves.*

Makeda listened. Always, she listened. From behind carved screens, from shadowed corridors, from the balcony above the temple. What she heard was not only sorrow—it was ambition. Men shifted like wolves in the dark, waiting for the king's breath to falter.

But she also heard her father call for her in the stillness of night. He would sit with her beneath the stars, pointing at constellations and tracing their names in the sky.

"You are not a boy," he said once, voice rough. "But you have eyes keener than any hawk and ears that drink truth from silence. The throne must follow blood. And if blood has chosen you, then you must be ready."

Her throat ached. "They will never accept me."

"Then make them unable to do otherwise," he whispered, the echo of his words from the night of the incense trial.

In the days that followed, she trained in silence. She watched the generals argue about raiders, the priests debate about sacrifices, the merchants clamor over trade. She marked where their loyalties bent, who lied smoothly, who sweated when they did. She learned who might stand with her and who would sharpen knives in the dark.

Weeks turned into months, and Makeda changed with them. No longer content to hide behind the cedar screens, she began to walk the outer courtyards where officials gathered before entering the hall. She would pause to ask a pointed question or listen to the gossip that spilled more truth than a sworn oath. Her presence unsettled some, intrigued others. More than once, she caught a merchant cutting short a boast when he noticed her standing nearby, eyes calm but unblinking.

She sought out the women of the palace too—servants, concubines, wives of nobles—learning from their whispers what the men would never confess in open court. From them she learned which captain spent coin faster than he earned it, which priest kept a mistress in the city, which merchant had quietly shifted allegiance to Egypt's envoys. She tucked each detail away, weaving a map of power invisible to anyone else.

At night, she walked the gardens with her father. His steps slowed, his voice thinner, but his mind still sharp. He tested her with riddles, counseled her with proverbs, and asked her to judge small disputes brought privately before him. "Not every quarrel belongs in the hall," he would say. "But every quarrel teaches you how men will grasp for advantage."

Makeda grew into the role that loomed before her, though she never named it aloud. She practiced the stillness of her father's listening, the steel of his patience, the quiet authority that could silence a room without raising a hand.

But the seasons turned, and with each one her father's vigor ebbed. The man who had once hunted lions could no longer mount his horse. His laughter came less often, his meals grew smaller, his eyes seemed always fixed on some far horizon.

When her father's strength waned and he was carried to his bed, she knew the hour was near. She sat with him until his final breath, his hand clasped in hers, the old lotus amulet between them.

And when the wailing began anew, and the throne stood empty with its lion's feet glinting in the lamplight, Makeda stepped into the hall. Not as a girl in the shadows. Not as the sister of the fallen heir.

But as the woman the kingdom would either crown...or devour.

Chapter Three

The Crown Descends

T he throne room smelled of frankincense and iron.

Her father's body had scarcely been laid in the tomb when the council convened, summoned by bells that echoed like thunder through the city. The lion-footed chair stood empty, draped in black cloth, its golden sheen muted in the lamplight. Around it gathered the kingdom's power: generals in stiff leather and bronze, priests in white linen with lapis at their throats, merchants in silks fragrant with spice.

Makeda entered barefoot, her garments of mourning simple, her long hair braided in a crown close to her head. Her stride was quiet, measured, yet the hall shifted as she passed—as though a shadow of her father's presence had returned in another form. She was not adorned, not crowned, yet there was a light about her that could not be hidden by plain linen.

It was Haran, the merchant once caught padding his ledgers, who spoke first. Of course it was. His voice rang out smooth and confident, sharpened on self-interest.

"The Lion is gone," he said, spreading his jeweled hands as if in blessing. "The gods have claimed him. We must not dishonor his legacy with disorder. His son is gone also, may the heavens receive him. Therefore—" His gaze swept the hall and settled on Makeda, dismissive as a hand brushing ash from a cloak. "We must choose a worthy man to sit the throne. Perhaps one from a noble house. Perhaps one bound by blood to Egypt, whose strength would steady our borders."

Murmurs rippled through the hall like wind through dry reeds. A few heads nodded. The priests bent toward each other, whispering.

Makeda stood still. She let them speak. She let their words fill the hall, every doubt, every argument that a woman could not rule. She let the tide rise high enough that when she struck it would crash louder.

A general cleared his throat. "With respect, Majesty's daughter is clever and well-loved in the women's court, but—" He faltered when her gaze cut to him, direct as an arrow. For an instant he seemed to see not a grieving daughter but a queen-in-waiting, her eyes bright and un-wavering above skin as flawless as silk. "But war and trade are the work of men. The people will not march behind a woman."

Another voice chimed in from the priests: "It is not the custom. The gods have always favored kings, not queens. To seat her on the throne would invite their wrath."

Haran smiled faintly, satisfied. "Better to decide swiftly, before disorder comes. Let us name a council regent until Egypt sends us a prince. A man to steady the ship until the waves calm."

Makeda took a step forward, and the sound of her heel striking stone rang like a hammer on an anvil. The hall fell into uneasy silence.

"Enough," she said.

The word cracked through the chamber like lightning.

She walked to the lion-footed chair and laid her hand on its carved arm. Her mourning linen shifted against her skin, black against gold. She did not sit—not yet—but her presence beside the throne made it plain: the chair was hers, whether they willed it or not.

"You speak of the gods' wrath," she said, her voice low but carrying. "Were you there when my father judged men who cheated the temple itself? Did you see the smoke of false incense crawl sideways, heavy with deceit? The gods revealed the truth through him then, and through me, before he ever spoke. If the gods disapproved of me, why would they have given me eyes to see what you men missed?"

Haran shifted, but she did not look at him. She raised her chin, the braided crown of her hair gleaming faintly in the lamplight, her posture so regal that for a moment even her critics drew back.

"You claim the gods will not bless a queen. Show me the law that binds them. Show me the scripture carved in stone. If you cannot, then you speak only your fear, not the will of heaven."

Her gaze swept to the generals, hard as steel. "And you—would you have a council of merchants lead your armies? Would you bend your knee to Egypt, begging for a prince to guard your wives and your wells? My father taught me patience. But he also taught me this—" She snatched a spear from the guard nearest her, its bronze tip flashing in the lamplight. She drove it into the stone floor beside the throne with a crack that echoed through the chamber. "—a kingdom divided is a kingdom already bleeding."

The hall went still. Even the braziers seemed to hold their breath.

Makeda's voice softened, but it burned no less fiercely. "I am my father's blood. I have sat in these shadows, listening, learning, when you thought me nothing more than a girl. I have seen where your loyalties bend. I know who would sell us to raiders, who would bow to foreign kings, who would drain the wells dry for their own gain. Do not think I will forget it."

She let the silence stretch until every man felt its weight. Then, finally, she lowered herself into the lion-footed chair.

The mourning cloth shifted, and the gold of the throne blazed once more in the lamplight.

Makeda sat as though she had always belonged there.

"This kingdom is not a ship to be steadied by a regent," she said. "It is a lion. And today, it has a queen."

No one spoke. Even Haran's tongue failed him. The priests lowered their eyes. The generals exchanged wary glances.

The crown had not yet been set upon her head, but in that moment, Makeda knew: it was hers.

Chapter Four

The Weight of the Crown

The throne of Sheba was carved of dark wood, high-backed and crowned with lions whose golden eyes glinted in the torchlight. Upon it Makeda sat, the diadem of her fathers newly upon her brow. The court shifted uneasily at first—men unaccustomed to bowing before a woman—but her gaze silenced hesitation.

Petitions came. A merchant accused of cheating scales. A farmer whose well had been seized by his neighbor. A widow pressed for tribute she could not pay. Makeda listened, head inclined, hands folded, her face as still as carved ivory. She asked questions the elders had not thought to ask, drew out truth with patience and sharpness both, and when she delivered judgment, her voice was steady as stone.

"Return the well. Pay back the measure stolen. And let none lay hand upon a widow's roof so long as I reign."

The murmurs of approval rippled through the court. Her father's counselors exchanged glances, some with grudging respect, others with calculation. Makeda saw it all and tucked it away. Ruling was more than speaking law; it was measuring hearts.

Yet when court dismissed and the lamps burned low, she did not rest easy. She walked the palace colonnades, the desert wind stirring her veils, and thought of the burdens on her shoulders. A queen's word could raise or ruin, heal or wound. Was her wisdom enough?

It was then the rumors reached her.

Traders from the north spoke of a king in Jerusalem whose wisdom surpassed all others. They told of judgments that turned snares into justice, of proverbs spoken like pearls, of a Temple unlike anything in the world—where the God of Israel Himself was said to dwell.

"Solomon," they whispered, and even hardened caravaners lowered their voices as though the name carried weight.

Makeda's eyes narrowed in thought. She had heard many boasts of kings before—some born of truth, others inflated with dust and vanity. But this name lingered. Not merely for his wealth or power, but for the word that clung to him: *wisdom.*

That night she stood at her window, gazing north into the vast dark. "If he is as wise as they say," she murmured, "then I will know it. I will test him as none has tested him before. And if he is truly a fountain of wisdom, perhaps I will drink enough to strengthen my people."

Her decision settled like stone. She would go—not as supplicant, but as sovereign. To measure Solomon's mind, to weigh his heart, and perhaps, to learn.

Chapter Five

Israel's Golden Reign

J erusalem woke glittering.

From the Mount of Olives the city looked like a bowl of light—terraces of pale limestone stepping down to narrow streets, courtyards brimming with fig and pomegranate, roofs hung with drying flax and bright dyed cloth that stirred at the slightest breeze. Pilgrims climbed the steps to the temple with offerings tucked to their hearts. Traders jostled by the Fish Gate, arguing in three tongues at once over salt and cedar and Tyrian purple. And above it all rose the House of the Name—cedar-beamed and gold-bright, its doors banded with bronze lilies, its inner courts humming with psalms and the rhythmic slap of priestly sandals.

They said wisdom lived here now, as if it were a person who had chosen a dwelling.

They meant Solomon.

He was not on the high throne when the petitioners were summoned but in the lower garden court, where shade pooled beneath an arbor of grape and jasmine and water spoke softly from a lion-mouthed fountain. Guards ringed the space at an easy distance, bronze catching the sun. Scribes waited beneath awnings with reed pens ready, knives tucked behind their ears for sharpening. Courtiers stood in the penumbra of the king's favor, practicing the art of appearing both attentive and invisible.

Two women faced him at the fore, every line of their bodies tight as bowstrings. One was thick-waisted, hair half-loosed from its pins; fury had reddened the delicate skin beneath her eyes. The other was narrow-shouldered and trembling, a thread of a woman who looked as if anger would break her. Their words collided midair, each insisting, each pleading. Between them, swaddled and blinking against the brightness, lay a baby with a shock of dark hair and a mouth that searched sleepily for milk.

Solomon listened as if nothing else in the world required his attention.

Up close, he did not radiate the cold, distant sanctity some imagined in a judge. He looked more like a man who enjoyed being alive. The lines at the corners of his eyes came as much from laughter as thought. The sun had written itself into his skin; his forearms, bared below the sleeves of a simple linen tunic, were strong and lightly scarred from youth spent in labor and sport. His beard was kept short along a jaw that could soften quickly when he smiled and harden just as quickly when he did not. But it was his gaze that unsettled men—a steady, unhurried assessment that made pretense feel suddenly childish. To be looked at by Solomon was to be weighed without warning.

"Majesty," the thicker woman said, with a convincing wobble. "We shared a house, this one and I. I bore a son, and the next day she bore one also. In the night her child died. She exchanged our infants while I slept and claimed mine as hers. When I said, *No, the living is my son,* she called me liar. I beg you—give me back what is mine."

The slender woman's hands knotted in her robe. "He is mine. I would cut my heart from my breast before I lied here."

Scribes whispered to one another and began to note the phrases that might be saved to proverb later. A warm wind shifted the jasmine, carrying sweetness through the court. Somewhere in the women's chambers a lute sounded—a practice scale, a missed note, a giggle.

Solomon gestured for the guards to bring the women closer. He asked them to recount their stories again, but differently—begin at the end, now at the beginning; tell the same tale without the details that flattered them, with only the things any neighbor might have seen. He asked questions that had nothing to do with babies or grief. *Which door faces the sun? Which servant slept in the inner room that night? Who first brought water in the morning?* He watched not their mouths but what happened to their faces when they lied.

When they had no more to say that could be said, he fell quiet.

"Bring me a sword," he said.

It was not shouted. He might have requested a cup of wine. The captain of the guard still flinched. Metal rang softly as a blade slid from a sheath, and the afternoon light laid itself along the length of it—white, clear, dazzling.

"Divide the child," Solomon said. "Half to each."

The slender woman fell to her knees so fast her bones struck stone. A sound tore out of her that made the scribes stop writing. "No!—no, my lord. Give him to her. Only let him live."

The other woman's mouth pinched tight, then opened on a cool little shrug. "It is just," she said. "Neither mine nor hers."

Solomon's hand lifted; the sword halted in air. He breathed out once, as if easing a door shut. "Give the child to the one who begged for his life," he said, voice like water finding its level. "She is his mother."

The fountain spoke again. Leaves clicked softly. A dove landed on the arbor and cooed. Then noise returned all at once—the intake of breath from courtiers, the low *ah* from the watching women at the edges, the murmured *He has judged...he has judged well*, the rustle of the scribes' frenzy to catch the exact words.

The true mother gathered her child, pressing him against her cheek the way a thirsty person embraces shade. The other woman—whose face had learned how to be innocent—went pale and thin, like smoke in a wind. The guards led her away gently, as if in this place even guilt deserved softness.

Solomon's expression, which had been bright with certainty a heartbeat ago, went tender as he watched the baby's small hand splay against his mother's neck. Something unguarded moved behind his eyes, and then was veiled again, as deftly as a woman drawing a curtain at noon.

He stood and the court stood with him. Favor petitioners filed forward: a dispute over an olive terrace and the way a stream jumped its bank in winter; a caravan master wanting redress after a Tyrian captain shaved the measure on his copper rods; A guard stepped forward to plead for a young widow. Her bridegroom had died before the wedding feast. She still held his dowry, Majesty, but not the house it was meant to repair.

Solomon heard them all, not hurrying even when the sun climbed toward its hottest point. He sent two matters to the temple, three to the market adjudicators, one to the captain of the city watch with instructions that made the captain blink, then grin. He settled another with a single question so simple the quarrelers blushed for not having asked it themselves.

By midafternoon the air swam. The scent of crushed mint rose where servants had spread branches on the paving stones to cool them. The scribes' jars of ink had grown thick; they thinned them with careful dribbles of water. The king's table in the shade bore untouched bread, a dish of goat cheese like fallen moons, figs sweating syrup. He broke one and ate without noticing.

"Majesty," said Benaiah son of Jehoiada, captain of the host, bowing. His voice had the scratch of a man more accustomed to shouting over wind and horses than speaking under arbors. "The northern road runs clean again. Your decoys did the work. We netted twelve bandits and chased the rest into hills where they will learn to love rocks. But there is talk beyond the Jordan of a war leader with more cleverness than appetite. I would like leave to meet him before he finds love for our wells."

"Take it," Solomon said, eyes on a parchment a scribe had held back for him—a sketch of a new aqueduct, gravity teased across stone and time to bring water to a dry quarter of the city. "Offer him a better road to wealth than raiding. If he sees profit he may decide he has always despised stealing."

Benaiah's brow furrowed. "And if he does not?" He liked answers sharp as spearpoints.

"Then teach him that thirst is a poor counselor," Solomon said, looking up at last with a flash of teeth that was almost a smile. "But ask him first."

Benaiah thumped a fist to his chest and withdrew, wearing the baffled pride of a soldier who had been told to try mercy before violence but trusted by his king to do either well.

More petitioners. More answers. And between each, a breath.

When at last the court was dismissed, a hush fell that had nothing to do with fear. It was the exhale of a city that had been held gently by the back of the neck and set straight again. Men carried the morning's judgment ahead of them like torches into the streets; by sunset it would be recited as if it had always been a story, as if anyone might have guessed the true mother by the shape grief takes when it is real. Children would act it out with clay dolls in dust. By tomorrow, a proverb would appear in two forms—one that fit the mouth easily and one that made the heart labor a little.

Solomon stayed where he was, alone at last under the arbor. The shade had thinned; sunlight dappled him in coins. He tipped his head back to look at the latticework of vine and sky. A goldfinch pecked the grapes just beyond his reach and scolded him for being a man.

From the women's pavilion drifted the scent of sandalwood and some rare perfume that had come tucked deep in a Phoenician chest—amber melted with resin, a hint of lemon. Laughter came and went, lifted and lowered like a veil. The king's household was a nation by itself, with its politics, its loyalties, its rituals of song and dance. Beauty here was not in short supply; it crowded the corridors and spilled across cushions. He had chosen and been given; he had been tempted and he had declined; he had been delighted and he had been bored. Wisdom, he had discovered, was no guarantee against loneliness. Sometimes it made the emptiness ring clearer, like a struck bowl.

A boy approached with a lyre cradled like a sleeping animal. He began to play without being asked—a simple tune at first, the kind mothers sing before the lamp is doused. Solomon's shoulders eased. Word-craft rose in him, the familiar itch in the mind's fingers.

He spoke softly, more to the fountain than to the boy:

"How bright is a word fitly spoken, like apples of gold in settings of silver. Better a little with peace than storehouses filled and a quarrelsome heart."

The scribe who had remained—an old man with hands stained the permanent brown of long ink—made a small sound of pleasure and wrote as fast as he could, his face alight as if the sun had reached him at last.

"Majesty," he said when the king fell silent, "do you ever tire of being quoted?"

Solomon smiled and did not answer.

A shadow moved at the garden's edge. It was Zadok the priest, white linen luminous even in shade. He bowed slightly, not as to a king but as to a friend.

"The morning's judgment will be a lamp for a long time," he said.

"Until men find a way to forget it," Solomon answered. "They are good at that."

Zadok's mouth tilted. "Then we will remind them."

They spoke for a moment about the temple—about the offerings, the firepans used for incense, and the great bronze pillars at its entrance, Jachin and Boaz, which still bore dust from the last storm.

Zadok's talk of holy things stitched the afternoon to the morning, temple to garden, God to king. When he had gone, Solomon remained still, as if he hoped the priest's quiet certainty might linger.

A servant appeared with a sealed tablet—the wax impressed with the stylized curve of a ship and a cedar tree, the sign of Hiram of Tyre. Solomon cracked it and read of wood shipments and skilled artisans, of purple-dyed cloth and a rumor tucked like a thorn at the end: caravans from the South thick with spice and gold, led by a queen who asks riddles of men and is disappointed when they answer.

He read the last line again, tasting the shape of it. A queen who asked riddles. He had known women who painted their mouths carnelian and spoke nothing that was not already someone else's thought. He had known women who could make a room forget itself with a look and had never once asked a real question. A queen who set trials before those who approached her—he felt the smallest shift inside his chest, like a door breathing in a house when the wind changes.

"Send Hiram our thanks," he told the scribe. "And ask him to tell me more of this southern queen, though I would prefer his facts to his poetry."

"Yes, my lord."

The sun slid lower. Long shadows of cypress and man bent together across the paving. The day's heat began to leak away into the ordering cool of evening. The boy with the lyre had drifted to sleep where he sat, hand fallen open on the strings. They breathed in sympathetic sleep, the instrument and the child.

Solomon stood and let his hand brush the boy's hair. He walked to the fountain, set his palms against the lion's bronze mane, and closed his eyes. The metal was hot from sun; it gave back the day's heat the way a loyal hound returns to its master. He could feel, far beneath his feet, the press of ancient water moving through stone—an old promise lifted from rock and brought to a thirsty hill.

He had everything a man could want and the knowledge that "everything" was never enough. He had a city that sang his name and an ear that strained sometimes for any voice that did not lower itself before him. He had wisdom that could part lies from truth like a knife parts fruit—and no one to hand the best slices to simply because he wished to see her mouth curve when she tasted.

He opened his eyes and looked toward the steep southern road that fell away from Jerusalem like a ribbon dropped from a table. Dust hung there far off, a smear against the sky. It might have been a caravan or a shepherd or nothing at all.

Still, he watched it longer than he meant to, as if waiting for a story to crest the horizon and arrive with the evening wind.

Chapter Six

A Song of Solitude

The palace grew hushed when the sun fell.

By day its courtyards rang with hammers on bronze, women's laughter spilling from silk-draped rooms, the thud of sandals and clatter of tongues in a dozen languages. But when the lamps were trimmed low and the last of the singers folded her harp, silence stretched across the stone like a cloak. Only the whisper of fountains and the faint cry of jackals beyond the wall reminded the king that the world still breathed.

Solomon lay awake beneath embroidered linen, staring at the carved beams of his chamber. The cedar wood had been hauled from Lebanon by ship, planed smooth and set in place by hands chosen for their skill. Gold leaf gleamed faintly in the lamplight, catching at the edges of inlaid lilies and pomegranates. The work was flawless.

And yet the perfection mocked him.

He rose, bare feet whispering over cool tiles, and walked to the terrace. From there Jerusalem spread below him, silvered by moonlight. The temple gleamed even at night, its gilded roof catching the stars. Beyond the city, the hills rolled dark and quiet.

He should have felt satisfied. He had built what his father David had only dreamed: a house for the Lord, a palace for his people, peace on every border. His coffers overflowed with tribute; his scribes had filled scroll upon scroll with his proverbs. Men said no question could outwit him, no riddle remain unanswered in his presence.

But wisdom carried a hidden tax: solitude.

He could share his throne, his bed, his wealth, but not the weight of understanding. The women who smiled for him had beauty enough to dazzle nations, yet too often their talk was rehearsed, their laughter practiced. Few dared to challenge him. Fewer still had the wit to match him.

Solomon turned, catching his reflection in a bronze mirror set in the wall. The man who gazed back was still in the strength of his years. His shoulders were broad, his frame tall, his face cleanly carved as though the chisel of heaven itself had taken care with its lines. His hair, dark as night with only the faintest threads of copper at the temples, framed eyes that glowed deep and steady, eyes that men found piercing and women found difficult to turn away from. He was, by any measure, a king both powerful and handsome.

And yet he looked at himself and saw only a man who longed for someone who could see past all of that.

He reached for the writing table, unrolling a strip of parchment. The words came almost without bidding, spilling from the hunger of his heart:

Tell me, whom does my soul seek? The courts are filled with beauty, yet none that stills the restless wind within me. I build palaces, but find no rest in their shade. I drink from golden cups, but thirst returns in the night.

He set down the pen, reading the lines by lamplight. The ache in them was sharper for being true. A man who could judge between women with a sword still could not still the longing in his own heart.

Outside, a caravan bell faintly chimed somewhere in the valley. He looked southward into the night, as if the sound itself had tugged at him. There was dust on the horizon, though it might be nothing more than wind. Still, he lingered at the balustrade until the moon climbed high, wondering why the thought of faraway lands stirred him more than all the comforts near at hand.

He returned to bed only when dawn threatened, the half-finished lines still glistening wet on the parchment.

Chapter Seven

Pondering the Rumors

The palace had gone still, yet Makeda's chamber glowed with the warmth of lamps and laughter. She had summoned her closest companions—three women who had walked beside her since girlhood, who dared to tease her where others bowed too low to speak.

They lounged on silk cushions strewn across the floor, bare feet peeking from linen robes, bracelets glinting in the firelight. The air was sweet with wine and roasted almonds, with a hint of rose oil cooling on their wrists. For one night, the crown felt lighter, the weight of tomorrow softened by the presence of friends.

"So," teased Tirzah, the boldest of them, leaning forward with a smile as sharp as her anklet bells, "you ride at dawn to meet the man they say has more concubines than soldiers. Are you sure, Majesty, that there will be any part of him left unclaimed?"

Makeda laughed, rich and unguarded. "If half the tales are true, he must be exhausted already. Perhaps I go only to see if he can still stand upright."

The women dissolved into laughter, covering their mouths like guilty girls.

"But they say he is handsome," another whispered, her eyes wide, her tone part envy, part wonder. "Dark hair, strong shoulders, a gaze that makes even queens lower their eyes. And clever—clever enough to answer any question before it is fully asked."

Makeda plucked a date from the platter, breaking it open with graceful fingers. "Handsome men are not so rare. Clever ones, rarer still. But a man who is both..." She lifted the fruit to her lips, pausing long enough to make them giggle again. "That is worth a journey."

"And what if the rumors are true?" Tirzah pressed. "What if he is a man who collects women as easily as others collect coins? Will you let yourself be numbered among them?"

Makeda's smile curved, slow and secret. "I am no man's number. If Solomon thinks to add me to his tally, let him first answer my riddles without stumbling. Let him prove he is more than appetite dressed in gold."

Her friends shivered with delight, nudging one another. "She will undo him," one whispered.

But when the laughter faded, Makeda sat back against her cushions, the firelight painting her skin in bronze and shadow. She was queen, fierce and commanding, yet her heart beat faster at the thought of a man who might meet her not with fear or flattery, but with equal fire. The stories of his beauty stirred her, yes—but it was the possibility of his mind, sharp and unyielding, that quickened her pulse.

When the last lamp was dimmed and her friends slipped away with whispers of farewell, Makeda lingered by the window. The desert night wrapped her in its cool breath, stars blazing like a thousand watchful eyes.

"Solomon," she murmured, half-challenge, half-confession. "They say you are wiser than all men and more handsome than most. Tomorrow, we shall see if your reputation is flesh—or only smoke."

Chapter Eight

First Sight of Jerusalem

Jerusalem had seen many processions. Envoys from Tyre with their ships' cargoes of purple cloth, Egyptian princes with gold harnesses flashing in the sun, even Babylonian scribes who carried scrolls so heavy they needed two men to lift them. But nothing like this.

The watchmen on the southern hills were the first to cry out. A line of dust moved across the horizon, long and shimmering in the heat. At its head marched spearmen with shields polished like mirrors. Behind them came a river of camels, their saddles draped in crimson, their bridles jingling with silver bells.

The air itself grew thick with fragrance. Sacks of cinnamon and cassia were slung across camel backs, spilling their sweetness into the wind. Great baskets of dried myrrh and frankincense resin were piled high, their pale tears glittering like pearls. Alabaster jars of perfumed oil were strapped in padded crates, dripping a faint trace of honeyed smoke into the dust. Tusks of ivory rose like pale banners, while bolts of indigo-dyed cloth rippled like captured sky.

And at the center, high upon a litter of carved ebony borne by attendants in white, rode a queen.

Makeda.

Her skin glowed the warm hue of honey poured in sunlight, smooth and flawless beneath the desert sky. Her hair, not bound in braids as the court expected from a queen of the South, tumbled in loose waves about her shoulders, soft and glistening as silk. A simple band of gold crowned her brow. Her teeth gleamed white in her smile, her lips full and sculpted, and her eyes—bright with wit, framed by thick lashes—were the kind that pierced a man's soul.

The people of Jerusalem lined the streets, craning for a glimpse. Some murmured blessings, others gaped in silence, as though they feared she might vanish if they breathed too loudly. Children darted forward to touch the hems of her attendants' robes, then ran back laughing, their hands scented faintly with myrrh.

From his palace balcony, Solomon watched.

He had been told of her splendor, but words had not prepared him. He had expected magnificence, of course—the wealth of Sheba was legend. He had even prepared himself for beauty. But this... this was different. She carried herself not as a woman paraded to impress, but as a sovereign who belonged above all eyes. Each gesture was measured, each glance deliberate, her dignity woven so tightly into her being that even the jewels at her throat seemed secondary.

Yet beneath the crown and veils, her mouth curved with the faintest suggestion of a smile—playful, knowing, as if she alone remembered the private jest she had shared with her friends the night before embarking on her voyage.

Solomon's hand tightened on the balcony rail. He was a king used to being sought, admired, bowed before. Yet watching her, he felt for the first time in years that he was the one being measured.

The horns of the temple sounded, long and low, welcoming her caravan through the gates. The echo rolled across the valley like a wave. Makeda's gaze lifted to the sound, and in that moment her eyes found his.

It was only a heartbeat, a passing glance across distance and noise and sunlight. Yet it held.

Solomon's chest stirred with something unexpected—a flare of curiosity, quickened by admiration, sharpened by desire. This was no rumor of wisdom, no whisper of beauty carried by caravans. This was a queen in flesh and flame, and she had come to test him.

And if the fire in her eyes matched the rumors of her riddles, then perhaps—for the first time in his reign—he had found his equal.

Chapter Nine

A Queen's Challenge

The throne room of Solomon was unlike any Makeda had ever seen.

She had walked beneath the gates of Egypt, where pylons soared into the sky and walls blazed with painted gods. She had stood in Saba's incense halls, where pillars were carved with vines and beasts. But here—here the very air seemed heavy with gold.

Cedar beams arched high above, their carvings alive with lilies and pomegranates. The floor was paved in gleaming stone, veins of silver glinting like rivers of light. Six steps rose to the throne itself, guarded by lions of carved ivory, their eyes set with precious stones. And upon the throne sat the man she had come so far to see.

Solomon.

He did not rise at her entrance, nor did he avert his eyes. He sat straight-backed, robed in white that gleamed against his skin, the crown of gold a simple band upon his brow. His hair fell in dark waves to his shoulders, his beard trimmed but not overly groomed. There was nothing gaudy about him, yet he seemed to command the light.

Handsome—yes. More than handsome. There was a quiet power in the way he watched her approach, unblinking, as if the entire hall had narrowed to a line between his gaze and hers.

Makeda walked forward, head lifted high, her litter left behind, her crown a slender circlet of gold resting upon her head, its minimal embellishments only heightening the splendor of her face. She moved with the ease of one accustomed to the weight of eyes. Murmurs rippled through the crowd: *Her skin, her hair, her jewels, her perfume.* She let them murmur. She walked not for them, but for the man on the throne.

From the screened galleries above, a cluster of women leaned close, silks whispering as they pressed against the lattice to glimpse the newcomer. These were Solomon's wives, his favored concubines, his companions—each accustomed to seeing their beauty reflected in the king's eyes, each curious about the woman who had crossed deserts for his wisdom.

"Look at her skin," one whispered, eyes wide. "Golden-brown and smooth as poured honey. I have never seen such a glow."

"And her hair," another murmured. "Not bound tight, not covered. Loose curls like silk—does she not know how scandalous that looks?"

"She knows," said an older one dryly, adjusting her bracelets. "That is why she wears it so."

A ripple of laughter traveled through the gallery, low and quick as the flutter of wings.

"She thinks she is different," sniffed a younger concubine, though she did not look away. "The king has a hundred beauties already. He will grow weary of her as he does of us all."

"Perhaps," said another, her tone sly, "but weary is not the word for what I see in his eyes just now."

They all leaned closer. Below, Makeda swept into the hall, her scarlet veils stirring with each step, her posture so regal that every gaze followed her without permission. She did not bow as deeply as others did, and the women hissed softly at her daring.

"Did you see that?" one giggled. "She tilted her head as though he were the guest and she the host!"

"She has courage," admitted the eldest, her voice almost grudging. "Or folly. But tell me—do you not feel it? The room bends toward her, like reeds before the wind. Even we, who have shared his nights, cannot draw such silence."

The younger ones hushed. For a heartbeat, they too felt it: the weight of Makeda's presence, the beauty that was more than skin or smile, the power of a woman who was not merely ornament but sovereign.

And when Solomon's laugh later rang out in answer to her bold words, the women in the gallery exchanged glances that glittered sharper than jewels.

"She will not be dismissed like the others," one whispered.

"No," said the eldest again, eyes narrowing with something that was not quite envy and not quite admiration. "This one is different."

At the foot of the throne steps, Makeda paused. Attendants shifted uneasily, waiting to see whether she would bow.

Makeda inclined her head—just enough to acknowledge a fellow sovereign. Not enough to suggest submission.

A smile flickered, quick as lightning, across Solomon's mouth. He had understood the gesture exactly.

"Welcome, Queen of Sheba," his voice carried easily, warm yet edged with curiosity. "You have traveled far, across deserts and dangers, to stand here. Tell me—what do you seek of Israel?"

Makeda's lips curved, full and deliberate. "I seek truth," she said. "The world speaks of Solomon the Wise, whose words turn quarrels into proverbs, whose judgments are sharper than swords. But I have heard many stories in my time. Not all stories carry weight."

A murmur, sharp this time. She had challenged him openly.

Solomon leaned one elbow upon the lion's carved arm. "And so you would weigh me, as a merchant weighs gold. Is that it?"

Her eyes gleamed. "If the gold is pure, it fears no scales."

The silence that followed rang like struck bronze.

Then Solomon laughed—deep, rich, unoffended. The hall exhaled with him. "Very well, Queen of Sheba. Test me, if that is your purpose. Bring your riddles, your questions, your treasures of wit and wealth. But understand this—" His eyes locked with hers, steady and dark. "You may test Solomon, but Solomon will also test you."

Makeda's pulse quickened. She felt the weight of the hall, the burn of the torches, the countless eyes watching. Yet in that moment there was only him—handsome, brilliant, utterly certain. A man who did not flinch before her fire.

She smiled slowly. "Then let the testing begin."

Chapter Ten

Perfumed Bath and Whispers

The queen's arrival had left the throne room ringing like a struck bell, but Solomon, with a gesture, had ordered rest for her before any testing of wisdom. Servants led Makeda through shaded corridors of cedar and gold, past fountains that spilled silver water into marble basins, until at last they opened the doors of the women's quarters.

The chamber within was a world of perfume and silk. Bronze lamps hung like captured suns, their light softened by gauze. Cushions the color of rubies and lapis were heaped against carved couches. Incense smoked lazily from golden bowls, carrying the sweetness of frankincense and the bite of cinnamon. In the center, a great alabaster bath steamed with scented water, petals floating on its surface like scattered stars.

Makeda paused, her eyes sweeping the chamber. She was queen—she had bathed in luxury before—but even she drew breath at the richness of this place.

Concubines surrounded her, graceful as gazelles, their movements practiced yet curious. Some approached with smiles, some with eyes sharp as needles, all eager to study this stranger who had come so far for their king. They unfastened her veils with hands soft as silk, letting the scarlet cloth spill to the floor. Her golden circlet was lifted from her brow, her jewels unclasped one by one. The air thickened with murmurs as each layer of her travel garments fell away.

"Her skin," one whispered, voice hushed with awe. "Like cinnamon smoothed with honey."
"Too foreign," another said quickly, though envy sparked in her eyes. "The king will tire of such spice."

"Will he?" said a third, her laughter low. "You saw his eyes in the hall. They did not tire."

Makeda allowed them to fuss over her, standing tall, regal even in her nakedness. Her hair tumbled loose about her shoulders, curls glistening as they combed oil through them. She lowered herself slowly into the bath, the warm water rising to her shoulders, carrying with it the scents of lotus and rose. The petals clung to her skin, drifting like offerings.

Above the rippling surface, her white teeth flashed in a smile that was neither shy nor boastful but entirely her own. "You whisper as if I cannot hear you," she said lightly, her voice rich with amusement. "Do you speak of me, or of yourselves?"

The women froze, their laughter caught in their throats. Then one bold girl giggled. "We speak of the king, Majesty. Always the king."

Makeda reclined against the alabaster edge, letting the warm water soak away the dust of the road. Her lashes lowered, her lips curved.

"Then perhaps he and I shall give you more to whisper of before long."

The women gasped, then dissolved into laughter, some covering their mouths, others shaking their heads in disbelief. The boldness of the queen's words startled them, but her charm was undeniable.

They continued to tend her, rubbing fragrant oils into her arms, smoothing balm across her legs, twining strands of fresh jasmine into her hair. Yet the room felt changed, as though the queen herself had become the center of gravity, drawing everything toward her without effort.

By the time Makeda rose, water streaming from her skin, the gossip had fallen into silence. She was clothed in fresh linen, soft as clouds, her body perfumed with myrrh and cassia. Jewels were set again at her throat and wrists, though none outshone her natural splendor.

When she stepped from the chamber, the women watched her go with eyes that burned with envy, admiration, and perhaps, for the first time, respect.

Tomorrow, the riddles would begin. But tonight, Jerusalem itself seemed to bow beneath the arrival of a queen who could not be ignored.

Chapter Eleven

The Banquet of Gold

The great hall of Solomon's palace blazed with light.

Bronze braziers sent flames dancing against carved cedar walls; long tables groaned beneath dishes of roasted lamb, figs lacquered in honey, bowls of pomegranates split wide like jewels. Wine flowed in golden cups, and the sound of lutes and harps braided through the room with the sweetness of incense rising in pale ribbons toward the rafters. Courtiers in silks and merchants in bright foreign garb leaned close, their whispers weaving as thick as the smoke.

Makeda was seated at Solomon's right hand, a place no foreign sovereign had ever been given. Her chair was carved of ivory and inlaid with ebony, draped in scarlet that echoed her veils. The eyes of the hall never left her: some in admiration, some in suspicion, all in awe.

Behind her, tall and silent, stood two of her own guards—Ethiopian men in gilded cuirasses, their spears upright, eyes keen as blades. They did not move, save to breathe, but their presence spoke plainly: Makeda was no guest in need of protection. She had brought her strength with her.

Solomon lifted his cup and spoke, his voice carrying easily over the music. "This night we honor our guest, Makeda, Queen of Sheba, who has crossed deserts and rivers to stand within Jerusalem. May her wisdom enrich our own, and may her reign be long and untroubled."

The hall echoed with assent, but Makeda only raised her cup slightly, her smile a measured curve. "And may the famed wisdom of Israel prove more than a tale to weary travelers," she said, velvet-toned and edged with challenge.

A ripple of laughter moved through the guests. Solomon's brows arched, but his smile deepened. "Already the queen sharpens her blade," he said. "Should I fear for my reputation?"

"Fear?" Makeda let the word linger, eyes bright. "I would not counsel fear, my lord. But perhaps... readiness."

The courtiers leaned forward, delighted. It was rare to see their king teased so boldly, rarer still that he accepted it with amusement.

Plates were set before them: spiced quail, olives stuffed with almonds, flatbread perfumed with sesame. Solomon gestured for her to taste first. "Tell me, Queen of Sheba, does Jerusalem please your palate?"

Makeda broke the bread delicately, lips curving as she tasted it. "The bread is fine," she said, "but it is not the food that will satisfy me tonight."

Gasps fluttered around the hall like startled doves. Solomon's cup paused halfway to his lips.

For a heartbeat, Makeda let the silence hang. A spark flickered in her eyes; the faintest lift at the corner of her mouth confessed that she knew exactly how her words cut both ways—and she took quiet pleasure in the precision.

"And what does the queen hunger for?" Solomon asked, his voice low, though every ear strained to catch it.

"Answers," she said simply. "I have brought riddles as merchants bring wares. I intend to learn whether Israel's king is as quick of mind as men claim."

A murmur ran through the room, half excitement, half disbelief. Solomon laughed, warm and unoffended. "Then bring them forth. I am eager to taste this feast of words."

Makeda leaned back, radiant in the lamplight, her full lips curving just enough to unsettle any man who stared too long. "All in good time," she said. "It would be ungracious to starve a king before the last course is served."

Laughter burst bright as cymbals; the musicians answered with a flourish. Dancers entered—anklets chiming, veils floating like dawn mist—while servants poured wine the color of garnets. Yet for all the spectacle, the power in the hall ran like a taut, invisible thread between the two sovereigns at the high table.

Solomon inclined his head toward the musicians; a new melody rose, intricate and playful, echoing the turn and counterturn of their words. "If this night is a banquet," he said, "then wisdom shall be the spice."

"Then let us not be stingy with it," Makeda answered, eyes alight.

He smiled, pleased. "Tomorrow, then—the court assembled, the scribes ready, the temple horns sounding—Jerusalem will hear your questions and my replies."

"Tomorrow," she agreed. Her gaze held his, steady as a vow, bright as a dare.

Around them the feast roared on—silver platters borne aloft, laughter tumbling, music braiding through flame and perfume—but the true revelry was quieter: a meeting of equals, a game begun, a promise of words that would bite like cinnamon and linger like honey.

And somewhere above, behind a curtain of lattice, a knot of women watched and whispered, bracelets chiming like soft laughter, as the king and the queen set the table for a different kind of feast.

Chapter Twelve

The Queen's Riddles

Morning spilled gold over Jerusalem, washing the temple roof in fire and setting the palace lions aglow. Horns sounded from the outer courts—three long calls—and the city answered, streaming toward the great hall as if drawn by a tide. Scribes sharpened reeds. Priests murmured blessings. Merchants elbowed for a clearer view. Even the guards stood a touch taller, polished bronze bright as noon.

Solomon took his place upon the lion-footed throne, composed and radiant, white robes falling in clean lines, the golden circlet resting lightly on his brow. The stillness about him wasn't emptiness but readiness, like a bow, drawn and patient.

Opposite him, raised on a dais of gold and ivory, sat Makeda. Two of her Ethiopian guards stood behind her, spears upright, eyes keen. She wore fresh linen edged with saffron; jasmine threaded her loosened curls. Her skin, golden-brown and smooth as polished amber, gathered the light and gave it back in soft fire. She glanced once toward the latticed galleries above, where silk and bracelets whispered—Solomon's wives and concubines leaning forward to watch—and then she rose.

A hush fell into place like a stone set in a wall.

"Solomon of Israel," she said, voice smooth as poured oil, "men tell me your wisdom is without equal. Let us see whether the tale is truth or traveler's embroidery."

Solomon inclined his head. "Ask, Queen of Sheba. If wisdom is a lamp, it was not lit to be hidden."

Makeda smiled—not softly, not cruelly, but with the pleasure of a fencer saluting before the bout. She took a slow step, scarlet hem brushing the stone.

"First," she said, and her gaze did not waver from his, "*what is that which a man loves more than life, fears more than death or mortal strife; what the poor have, the rich require, and what contented men desire?*"

The riddle wound through the hall like incense, sweet and sharp. In the gallery, a young wife whispered, "Oh! I know it—no, I don't—hush!"

Solomon's mouth tilted, a quick, private light. "Nothing," he said.

The hall laughed and gasped as one; reeds scratched furiously. Makeda's lashes dipped, then lifted. "A simple blade, cleanly used," she said. "Well struck."

"Your hand was steady," he returned, and that earned the faintest color at the edge of her smile.

She paced again. "Another," she said, and her tone sharpened like a new edge. "*What rises with the sun yet never leaves the earth; has no voice yet speaks to all; and though it dies each night, is reborn with every dawn?*"

Heads turned to Solomon as if pulled by a cord. He did not look away from her. "A shadow," he answered, "faithful even to the faithless."

A ripple of approval passed through the hall; even the soldiers allowed themselves a small grin. Above, bracelets chimed as the women shifted.

"See how she smiles," one murmured behind the lattice, half envy, half delight. "And see how he looks at her," another breathed. "Hush," said the eldest. "Let them dance."

Makeda's smile deepened, a richer thing now, warmed by genuine admiration. "You are swift," she said. "Let us see if you are also deep."

She turned, letting the hall feel the silk of the pause, then faced him again. "*I am greater than kings and poorer than beggars. I devour iron and crumble stone. I am the patient end of rivers and the quiet thief of empires. Who am I?"*

The court held its breath. A merchant mouthed words silently, counting on his fingers, as if numbers might snare it. The priests frowned in pleasure. Above, a concubine whispered, "If he misses—" and did not finish.

Solomon rested his forearm on the carved lion's mane. For a heartbeat his gaze slid past Makeda to the open doors where light walked across the floor. When his eyes returned to her, they were bright.

"Time," he said. "What kings cannot bribe and beggars cannot lose."

The sound that followed was not mere noise; it was relief, delight, awe stitched together. Hands struck palms; feet stamped once, twice. The scribes looked dazed, as if the ink itself wanted to applaud.

Makeda's chin lifted—not in pride, but in pleasure that he had come so quickly to the heart. "You pay attention," she murmured. "Good." She let the word sit between them, then offered the smallest tilt of her head—a queen's thank you, and a woman's.

Solomon's eyes warmed. "Your questions are a feast," he said. "I am in danger of forgetting the food."

"Do not," Makeda said lightly. "You will need your strength." She glanced at the gathered nobles, then back to him. "One more for the morning—then we spare your scribes and feed your guests."

"Cruelty disguised as kindness," he said, amused. "Proceed."

Her gaze held his, bright and teasing, and the hall leaned forward as if the walls themselves had learned to listen. *"From the eater came something sweet; from the strong came something to eat. Name the sweetness born of strength, and tell me why men crave it."*

The priests exchanged quick, startled looks at the echo of an old tale. The riddle was layered—Scripture under proverb, memory under metaphor. Solomon's mouth softened, almost tender. This was a riddle first given by Samson ages ago and it showed her knowledge of the history of his people.

"Honey from the lion," he said. "Sweetness born in the ribs of strength. Men crave it because it is victory made gentle."

Makeda's breath caught so subtly only the women above—trained in such small things—noticed. The eldest concubine smiled, satisfied. "Ah," she whispered. "Now they speak the same language."

"True," Makeda said aloud. "And deftly answered." She let her hands rest lightly on the carved arms of her chair.

"Enough for morning. Even wisdom tires of being hunted."

Laughter eased the room; breath came back to chests. Attendants moved, pouring wine the color of garnets. Somewhere a drummer found a soft, pleasing rhythm. Still, the current between the two sovereigns did not slacken. It only settled, deeper, like a river after rapids.

Solomon rose a little, not quite standing—more an acknowledgment that the bout had paused, not ended. "Jerusalem thanks Her Majesty of Sheba," he said, the formal words carrying a thread of something personal. "We will reconvene at the next hour after the sun has passed the cedar's tip. If the queen is willing."

Makeda inclined her head. "The queen is willing. I have traveled far; I would not leave your mind half-measured."

"Nor I yours," he said, and the hall felt the smile in the words though his mouth barely moved.

Above, the women hummed with whispers. "She toys with him." "He toys back." "Which is hunter? Which is prey?" "Both," said the eldest, bracelets chiming. "And neither."

Makeda turned to step down from her dais; her guards shifted with her, perfectly timed. She paused, as if remembering something, and looked over her shoulder—not at the court, not at the women, but at Solomon alone.

"Tell me, my lord," she said, voice low enough that only the front ranks heard it and everyone else pretended they had, "*what has many tongues but never speaks, is bound yet travels, and in traveling, moves kings and markets alike?*"

He didn't blink. "A rumor," he answered. "Today's is that a queen has come who will not be satisfied until the truth wears no veil."

Her lips curved, slow and unmistakably pleased. "Then let us see how many veils truth owns," she said, and swept from the dais.

The court stirred back to life—wine poured, bread broken, laughter resumed—but the scribes' hands shook as they capped their ink. Outside, the horns called the next watch. Inside, two minds had met as evenly as blades, and the nick each had taken from the other glittered like a jewel.

By afternoon, the city would retell every word, embroidered and bright. By evening, new riddles would be minted in the market, sold for figs and traded for favors. And by nightfall, both king and queen would find that food had not dulled their hunger at all.

The duel had only begun.

Chapter Thirteen

The Duel Deepens

The second day dawned warm and cloudless, the pale stone of Jerusalem shimmering like ivory under the sun. Already the city hummed with anticipation. Merchants carried fresh tales into the markets: how the queen of Sheba had come not with armies but with riddles, how Solomon had answered each with ease, and how her smile—intoxicating as wine, bright as sunlight—had lingered longer than courtesy demanded.

By the time Makeda entered the hall, the crowd pressed tighter than the day before. Priests crowded beside scribes, merchants jostled for space behind soldiers. Even the women in the upper galleries had multiplied, silks rustling like birds in a fig tree. Their bracelets tinkled as they leaned forward, hungry to see if this day the queen might finally snare their king.

Solomon sat already upon his throne, calm as the sea at dawn. Makeda crossed the floor with unhurried steps, her guards at her back, her eyes bright and steady. The air seemed to shift around her; even the gossip of the concubines fell into silence when she lifted her chin.

She inclined her head just enough to honor him, then raised her voice. "My lord, yesterday you met my first riddles with answers sharp as the sword of David himself. But let us see if your wisdom is also deep. For there are questions no blade can cut."

A murmur moved through the chamber like wind through reeds. Solomon leaned forward slightly, one hand resting on the carved mane of the ivory lion. "Then test me, Queen of Sheba. If your words hold depth, I will dive for them."

Makeda's lips curved. "Tell me then: *What builds a house yet lives not within it; dies when given away, yet multiplies when shared?*"

The riddle hung in the air, simple and impossible all at once. Nobles frowned. A merchant whispered to his neighbor, "Gold builds a house—no, no, not right..." The women in the gallery whispered furiously, bracelets chiming.

Solomon's answer came quiet but sure. "Wisdom," he said. "It lays the foundation of a house, yet it does not dwell in stone. If a man keeps it to himself, it withers. But if he shares it, it multiplies."

The court exhaled as if one. The scribes' pens darted, catching each word before it fled.

Makeda let her lashes fall, then lifted them again, her eyes alive with satisfaction. "Good. Then try another: *What cannot be held in the hand, yet rules kings and beggars alike; is older than the mountains, yet is renewed each morning?*"

A priest pursed his lips; a soldier muttered. From the gallery came a whisper edged with laughter: "Ah, now she has him!"

But Solomon only smiled, his gaze fixed on Makeda. "The breath of life," he said. "It belongs to all, yet to none. When it departs, no man can command it. Each dawn it is given again, though none can say why."

The gallery fell silent. Even the women who had scoffed the day before pressed their hands to the lattice, watching the queen's face.

Makeda tilted her head, jasmine brushing her cheek. "You answer as though you knew my thoughts before I spoke them."

"Perhaps," Solomon said, "your thoughts are not so hidden as you think."

The court laughed, delighted by the boldness of his tone. Makeda's smile deepened, not offended but pleased. Her voice dropped, lower, velvet threaded with fire.

"Then let me set a sharper snare: *What is soft enough to soothe, strong enough to bind, invisible to the eye, yet felt more than iron chains?*"

The hall hushed. This was no riddle of shadow or stone, but of the heart. The gallery stirred; one concubine hissed, "She dares!" while another whispered, "Watch him now."

Solomon's eyes held hers, unblinking. The corner of his mouth lifted. "Love," he said simply. "It binds the free, softens the hard, and is seen only in its work. No chain is stronger."

For a heartbeat, no one moved. Then the hall erupted, applause like thunder, laughter rolling against the pillars.

But Makeda did not laugh. She smiled slowly, the kind of smile that revealed nothing and everything at once, and the look she gave him was not a queen's but a woman's—sharp, knowing, faintly dangerous.

"Perhaps you are wise indeed," she said.

Solomon inclined his head, eyes never leaving hers. "Perhaps you are cunning indeed."

The air between them shimmered like heat over stone. Around them, the feast resumed—music rising, goblets filled, servants moving—but the court knew it was watching more than riddles.

From the gallery, the eldest concubine leaned close to her companions. "Mark me well," she whispered. "The queen smiles too much. And the king—he listens too closely."

The formal riddles ended, but the morning did not. When the scribes set down their reeds and the courtiers drifted into conversation, Solomon rose from his throne and came to Makeda's side.

"Come," he said, his voice pitched low enough for her ears alone. "Let the court have their noise. You and I will have the city."

So it was that she found herself walking beside him through the cedar-pillared corridors, her guards trailing a respectful distance behind. The air grew fresher as they stepped out onto the terraces, where the sun spilled wide and golden over Jerusalem.

Below them stretched the king's gardens—terraces lined with palms, pools where lilies floated, vineyards climbing the slopes beyond the walls. Beyond that, the hills rolled green and tawny, studded with flocks that moved like white stones across the earth.

"Your kingdom is fertile," Makeda said, pausing to breathe in the scent of rosemary and fig. "The land itself seems to prosper under your hand."

Solomon's eyes crinkled faintly at the corners. "A king does not prosper alone. Wisdom builds, but it is the people who plant and reap. A king who forgets that soon finds his throne built on sand."

Makeda glanced sidelong at him, measuring the weight of the words. They were not flattery; they were truth spoken plain.

Her thoughts slipped backward, unbidden, across the years. To the cool shadows of her father's council hall, where as a girl she had crouched behind carved screens, listening to men argue about taxes and wars. To the nights when her father had called her close after her brother's death, resting a heavy hand on her hair and saying, "Wisdom is the only treasure a ruler cannot squander. Riddles teach you to see beneath words, and wisdom teaches you to see beneath men."

Her heart gave a small, painful twist. He had been right. Riddles were more than play; they were training, a map for ruling, a weapon sharper than steel. And here, walking the terraces of Jerusalem, she was testing that truth against the man the world called wisest.

Solomon gestured to the horizon where the temple gleamed, its bronze pillars shining. "When my father, David, died, he charged me to build the house of the Lord. Many doubted me then—too young, too untried. But wisdom makes a boy into a man, if he is willing to listen."

Makeda's lips curved faintly. "And do you listen still, my lord? Or does the world now listen only to you?"

He turned to her then, eyes dark and steady. "Today," he said, "the world listens to you."

Heat flickered low in her chest—not the heat of the sun, but of recognition. She looked away, letting her gaze rest on the lilies nodding in the pool. "Be careful, Solomon," she said softly. "My father taught me to hear not only words, but what lies beneath them. And sometimes... beneath them lies danger."

"Or desire," he countered, no louder than she had spoken.

The word hung between them, sweet and perilous.

Makeda lifted her chin, meeting his gaze again with the boldness of one who would not retreat. "Perhaps. But riddles are not solved in a single breath. They must unfold."

His smile was slow, deliberate. "Then let them unfold, Queen of Sheba."

They paused at the far end of the terrace, where the temple's gleaming roof dominated the view. Priests moved like white ants below, their chants drifting upward with the smoke of offerings.

Solomon gestured. "There stands the house of my God. All the wealth of Israel, all the labor of men, was poured into its making. Surely even a queen of Sheba must admit there is no temple greater on earth."

Makeda's gaze lingered on the bronze pillars, the gilded doors, the smoke rising against the sky. It was magnificent, yes—but the words pressed against her pride.

"No temple is greater than the devotion it holds," she replied, her voice even. "Splendor without spirit is only stone and metal. My people honor in simplicity what others build with gold."

For the first time, Solomon's smile thinned. "Then perhaps your people mistake poverty for humility."

Her chin lifted. "And perhaps Israel mistakes ornament for truth."

The words fell like flint on steel. The courtiers behind them shifted uncomfortably; even the guards exchanged glances. But Makeda did not look away, and neither did he.

At last, Solomon inclined his head slightly. "You speak boldly, Queen of Sheba."

"I was taught," she said, her lashes lowering, "that wisdom does not grow in silence."

He studied her a long moment, his expression unreadable, then turned back toward the hall. "Rest now," he said at last. "We will speak again when the sun declines."

Makeda inclined her head, but her heart beat too fast. She returned to her chambers in silence, her guards trailing behind.

When at last she was alone, she sank onto the cushions, jasmine still clinging to her hair. The day's riddles echoed in her mind—his ease, his brilliance, the way his dark eyes had kindled when he spoke of love. And yet, there on the terrace, he had stung her. He had shown pride, perhaps even arrogance, and she had answered with her own.

She pressed her hand over the lotus amulet at her throat, the one her father had given her. Wisdom is sharper than pride, he used to say. But wisdom did not stop the heat that lingered when she thought of Solomon's voice, or the way he had not looked away when she challenged him.

Makeda lay back, staring up at the carved cedar ceiling. She was queen, sovereign, no man's ornament. And yet... for the first time, she wondered whether wisdom alone would be enough to guard her heart.

Chapter Fourteen

The King's Questions

B y evening the hall was lit again with fire and music, but the mood was tauter than the night before. Servants hurried more quietly, nobles glanced sideways more often, and from the latticed galleries above, the concubines whispered eagerly, bracelets chiming like nervous bells. Word of the sharp exchange on the terrace had spread. Tonight, all Jerusalem waited to see whether king and queen would clash again—or something else entirely.

Makeda entered with her guards, her curls cascading and gleaming with jasmine oil. She moved with regal composure, yet beneath it she carried the memory of Solomon's words—ornament, truth, poverty, humility—each like a thorn pressed to her pride. She vowed not to yield ground tonight.

Solomon rose when she approached, the faintest smile tugging his mouth. He gestured to the seat at his right. "Queen of Sheba. Will you take wine with me again?"

She inclined her head and sat, her veil slipping just enough to show the curve of her lips. "So long as it is not poured with arrogance," she said.

The courtiers stiffened, half in shock, half in delight. Solomon only laughed, low and warm. "Then it will be poured with curiosity." He lifted the jug himself and filled her cup. "Tonight, it is my turn to ask."

Makeda arched a brow, tilting her cup before drinking. "Is a king so weary of riddles that he must steal a queen's game?"

"Not steal," Solomon said, his eyes glinting in the lamplight. "Return in kind. You came to test me, Makeda. But I would know what lies beneath your questions."

The court hushed, straining to hear.

He leaned slightly toward her, his voice smooth. "Tell me, Queen of Sheba—why did you not send an envoy, as other rulers do? Why ride across desert and river yourself, when your throne might have sent messengers enough?"

Makeda's lips curved. "Because wisdom does not travel well in saddlebags. And because I wished to see the man behind the tales."

Murmurs ran through the hall. Solomon's eyes narrowed slightly, but not in anger—in focus. "And what do you see?"

Makeda met his gaze directly, unflinching. "A king who answers quickly, perhaps too quickly. A man who knows the weight of power, yet still tastes of youth's pride."

Gasps fluttered like startled birds. Even the musicians faltered for a beat before finding their rhythm again.

Solomon's smile returned, slower now, edged with challenge. "And I see a queen who listens as if every word is a jewel—but wears her crown like armor."

Makeda let the words settle. Then she laughed, rich and low, the sound cutting tension like a blade yet leaving it sharper. "Better armor than chains, my lord."

"Ah," Solomon said softly, "but sometimes chains are made of flowers, and even queens wear them willingly."

Her eyes brightened, dangerous and amused. "And sometimes kings forget that flowers wither. Wisdom, at least, does not."

The gallery hissed and whispered; bracelets clinked like a thousand tiny cymbals. The courtiers shifted in their seats, half-thrilled, half-uneasy.

Solomon leaned back at last, breaking the taut line between them. He raised his cup. "To wisdom, then," he said.

Makeda touched her cup to his, her smile edged with defiance. "And to flowers that do not chain."

They drank, eyes locked over the rim.

The music swelled, and a troupe of dancers spun across the hall, their anklets chiming, their veils catching the torchlight. The courtiers turned to watch, but not the king and queen. Their eyes remained fixed on each other, the words of their toast still trembling in the air between them.

"Tell me," Solomon said, tilting his cup lazily, though the sharpness of his gaze betrayed the ease of his pose, "do queens of Sheba often joust with words, or is it a pleasure you reserve for Israel alone?"

Makeda let her lashes dip, then lifted them with deliberate grace. "We joust, yes. But few opponents last beyond a round. Perhaps Israel should be honored that her king has not yet fallen."

The court laughed, delighted. Solomon smiled, but his eyes stayed on hers. "And perhaps Sheba should be honored that her queen has found someone worth sharpening her tongue against."

The dancers twirled, silks unfurling, their movements quick as firelight. A hush fell in the gallery above as the women leaned closer, whispers trembling like moth wings.

"Careful," Makeda said, her lips curving, "or you may find your tongue dulled by mine."

"Then let it be dulled," Solomon answered smoothly. "Better dulled by a queen's wit than rusted in silence."

Gasps and laughter rippled through the chamber. The musicians, catching the rhythm of their duel, struck a bolder chord, the drums echoing like a heartbeat.

Makeda leaned back, resting her elbow lightly against her chair, her posture regal yet womanly, unguarded. "You press hard, my lord. Perhaps you mistake my presence for invitation."

Solomon's smile widened, dangerous and amused. "And perhaps you mistake my questions for pursuit. Can a king not be curious?"

Makeda's laughter rang low and rich. "Curious kings are dangerous."

"Dangerous queens," Solomon countered softly, "are irresistible."

The hall seemed to pause. Even the dancers slowed, their movements languid, as though drawn into the gravity between king and queen.

At last, Makeda lifted her cup once more. "Then let curiosity and danger feast together tonight."

Solomon touched his goblet to hers, his voice carrying just enough for the hall to hear. "And let Israel and Sheba learn what fire is born when steel strikes steel."

The toast rang like a challenge, and the court roared with approval. Above, the concubines whispered furiously, bracelets clattering as though even their silence could not contain the tension.

When the music swelled again, the king and queen did not speak further. They had said enough. The dance of words had ended, but every glance, every pause, was another step in a duet no one could mistake for anything but desire.

Chapter Fifteen

The Garden at Night

The banquet lingered long, but when the last goblets had been drained and the musicians' final notes curled into silence, Solomon rose. With a word and a gesture, the court was dismissed, though the courtiers lingered, reluctant to leave the charged air.

Makeda also rose, her guards shifting behind her, but Solomon held out a hand. "Walk with me," he said softly. Not command, not plea—something between.

She hesitated, then inclined her head. "Very well."

They passed through torchlit corridors and out into the gardens. The night was warm, the air scented with myrtle and roses, the pools glimmering with the reflection of stars.

A fountain spilled water in a silver arc, its sound a quiet music.

Makeda's gaze lingered there, at the fountain, the jeweled drops falling and breaking. Solomon noticed. "Does Sheba lack water," he asked, "that its queen stares at every pool?"

Makeda's lips curved faintly. "In Sheba, water is life itself. A drop weighs as much as a pearl. My people guard their wells as your people guard their temple."

"Then I shall guard your thirst while you are here," Solomon said, his tone light but edged with meaning.

Her lashes lowered, then lifted again, sharp as a blade. "Guard it, my lord? Or tempt it?"

He smiled at that, dark eyes glinting in the torchlight. "Perhaps both. A man does not know the measure of a woman until he sees what she thirsts for."

Her pulse quickened despite herself, and she turned from him, studying the roses climbing the lattice, their blossoms pale in the moonlight. "You turn everything into a riddle," she said. "Do you not tire of testing?"

"Do you?" His voice came low behind her, closer than before. "You crossed deserts to test me. And yet..." His breath stirred the jasmine woven in her hair. "...you stay, though the answers do not always please you."

Makeda turned then, slowly, her face lit by starlight, her eyes dark fire. "Perhaps I stay," she said, "because the questions grow more dangerous. And I have not yet decided if danger tempts me... or destroys me."

For a heartbeat, silence. The fountain whispered, the night birds called, the garden itself seemed to hold its breath.

Solomon's gaze dropped briefly, deliberately, to the curve of her lips before rising to meet her eyes again. "Perhaps," he murmured, "the two are the same."

Her chest rose once, sharp, before she looked away again, breaking the spell. "It is late," she said, though her voice was not steady. "I will return to my chambers."

"As you will," Solomon replied, his smile unreadable. He inclined his head, the gesture courtly, but his eyes lingered on her as though he already knew the ending to a riddle she had not yet spoken.

When she reached her chamber door, Makeda pressed her hand over the lotus amulet at her throat, steadying her breath. He had unsettled her again, more deeply this time. Not only with his wit, but with the way her own body betrayed her—pulse quick, breath shallow, a warmth curling low that had nothing to do with wine.

And worst of all—she could not decide if he had meant only to spar... or if he was already weaving some clever snare that would bind her more surely than chains.

Chapter Sixteen

Perfume and Petals

T he next morning, sunlight spilled pale and golden through the latticed windows of Makeda's chambers. Servants moved like shadows, laying out silks, steaming basins, jars of alabaster sealed with wax. The air grew thick with fragrance—rose, frankincense, cassia—until the queen's rooms themselves seemed to breathe perfume.

Makeda allowed herself to be guided to the marble bath that had been prepared for her. The water shimmered with petals, crimson and ivory, floating like tiny boats. Steam curled upward, carrying the sweetness of myrrh.

Concubines attended her—not with the careless chatter they used among themselves, but with a reverent hush, as if uncertain how near to step. One bold girl knelt to unfasten

Makeda's sandals, her head bowed. Another drew a comb of carved bone through the queen's long flowing curls, her fingers careful, awed by the softness of hair not bound as theirs so often was.

Makeda stepped into the bath, her movement slow, deliberate, as befitted a queen. The warm water closed over her, scented and silken. She reclined against the smooth alabaster, lashes lowering, her face serene. She did not need to command their respect; her very presence demanded it.

Still, whispers rose among the women as they worked fragrant oils into her skin, smoothing along her arms, her shoulders, the long lines of her legs.

"Did you hear them last night?" one murmured. "He toasts her as if she were already his."

"He watches her," another whispered back, envy curling sharp in her tone. "The king does not watch us so."

"Hush," said a third, older, wiser. "She is not like us. She is a queen. Do not measure yourselves against her."

Makeda opened her eyes, her lips curving faintly. "If you whisper of me, at least let me hear it clearly," she said, her voice smooth, unhurried.

The women gasped, then laughed softly, caught and unashamed. One knelt lower and said, "Majesty, we only say what is plain to see—that the king has never been so taken."

Makeda let the words hang, then smiled, slow and enigmatic. "Taken?" she said. "A wise man may admire a flame without burning his hand. Do not mistake a glance for a surrender."

The concubines exchanged glances, some smiling, some doubtful. Yet even as they anointed her with myrrh and bound her hair in fresh jasmine, their eyes shone with fascination.

When Makeda rose from the bath, water streaming from her smooth skin, she seemed to them more goddess than woman, untouchable yet radiant. They draped her in linen white as cloud, clasped gold at her wrists, fastened a chain of pearls at her throat.

And though the whispers lingered, none dared speak as she crossed the chamber floor, regal as dawn itself. For she was not concubine, not servant, not even guest. She was Makeda, queen in her own right, and the very air seemed to bend beneath her sovereignty.

When the women finished their work, they brought forth a polished disk of bronze set in an ivory frame, bright enough to capture her image. Makeda dismissed them with a glance, then leaned forward, studying her reflection in the mirror.

Her skin gleamed with oil, having the darkness of her father with the honeyed glow of her mother. The pearls at her throat glowed softly against it, her lips full and curved, her lashes casting shadows. The jasmine woven through her hair brushed her cheek, delicate, fragrant. She was every inch the queen her father had raised her to be—sovereign, radiant, unyielding.

Yet her gaze lingered on her own eyes, and in their depths she saw something unsettled. The echo of Solomon's laughter. The memory of his voice, low and steady, when he had leaned close in the garden. The boldness of his questions. The way his answers to her riddles had not only satisfied her mind but stirred something lower, more dangerous.

Her lips curved—not in surrender, but in self-knowledge. So be it, she thought. He is handsome. He is clever. And he has made my heart quicken. But that does not mean he has won me.

She straightened, turning away from the mirror. No, she was not easy prey. Not for Solomon, not for any man. If he sought to bind her, he would need more than riddles and glances. He would need to prove himself in ways even the wisest of kings might not expect.

And yet, as she turned away from the mirror, the scent of jasmine rising from her hair, she knew that the game was no longer his alone.

Chapter Seventeen

A Feast of Questions

The hall glittered once more with lamps and gold, the air thick with music and wine. Yet beneath the spectacle ran a taut thread only the boldest dared name: the queen of Sheba and the king of Israel, locked in a duel of minds and something more dangerous.

Makeda entered with her guards, hair falling loosely bound only be her slender golden circlet and jasmine, her skin gleaming from the morning's oils. She carried herself as though last night's garden walk had been no more than a polite tour, though her heart remembered his nearness, the way his words had lingered like heat on her skin.

Solomon rose as she approached, offering her the seat at his side. "Queen of Sheba," he said warmly, "Jerusalem feasts again in your honor. Will you share bread and wine with me?"

Makeda smiled, regal and untouchable. "Bread and wine I will take, my lord. But no more boasts about Israel's splendor—lest we spend another evening trading thorns."

The court chuckled nervously. Solomon's grin was slow, deliberate. "Then let us trade jewels instead." He leaned closer. "Your riddles against mine."

Her eyes lit, wary and amused. "You would test me in my own game?"

"Why not?" His voice was velvet, but edged. "Wisdom does not grow if it is never risked."

The court leaned forward as Solomon raised his voice, clear and rich: "Tell me, Queen of Sheba—*what is more precious than gold, stronger than armies, yet vanishes when a man opens his hand?*"

Makeda's brows arched, the faintest smile tugging her lips. She did not hesitate. "Trust," she said. "Hard to win, easy to lose. When it is gone, no king can summon it back."

Murmurs swept the hall. Solomon inclined his head, pleased. "Well answered. Another, then: *What fills every vessel yet is never seen; quenches thirst, cools fire, gives life, and takes it away?*"

At this the hall went still. The riddle coiled like smoke, familiar and dangerous. Above, in the gallery, the women leaned closer, whispering.

Makeda's eyes narrowed. She knew the answer. It was plain. Yet she heard the undertone in his voice, saw the glint in his eyes. He was playing deeper now, weaving the duel toward something else.

"Water," she said at last. Her voice was steady, but her heart stirred uneasily.

Solomon's smile was quiet, unreadable. "Yes. Water. The simplest treasure, and the one most easily taken."

Their eyes locked. A beat of silence pulsed between them, heavy with things unsaid. Then the hall erupted in applause, and the spell broke.

Makeda lifted her cup and drank, though it was wine, not water. Still, she felt the weight of his gaze, and for the first time she wondered if she had stepped into a riddle greater than her own.

The applause faded into the rise of music. Harps and pipes wove a bright melody, and dancers swept into the hall, their veils trailing like flames, their anklets chiming in rhythm with the drums. Servants moved deftly, setting platters of roasted lamb, bowls of honeyed figs, and cups brimming with spiced wine upon the long tables.

Makeda sat at Solomon's side, the scent of cinnamon and roasted almonds mingling with the jasmine in her hair. She felt the weight of his presence beside her—too near, yet not near enough.

"You play the riddler well," she said, her lips curving as she lifted her goblet. "But are you as skilled at feasting as you are at answering?"

Solomon leaned closer, his dark eyes catching the lamplight. "A feast without laughter is famine. Sit beside me and I will see to it that you lack nothing."

Her smile deepened, though she kept her gaze on the dancers. "Dangerous words, my lord. A queen who lacks nothing is difficult to impress."

"And yet here you are," he countered smoothly, "and still I try."

A platter of pomegranates was set before them, their jeweled seeds glistening. Solomon plucked one, its skin splitting under his thumb, and held a cluster toward her. Makeda hesitated only a moment before leaning close enough for her fingers to brush his as she accepted it. The spark of contact was small, but her pulse quickened.

"You tempt me with fruit, as though I were Eve," she said lightly, biting into the sweetness.

"And if you were?" Solomon's voice was low, threaded with humor. "Would Eden not be worth it?"

Her laughter rang out, rich and genuine, startling even her attendants. Yet she turned away before her smile grew too revealing, letting her eyes follow the dancers as they spun.

As the music quickened, couples rose to join in the circle. Makeda did not, but Solomon leaned nearer. "Do queens of Sheba not dance?"

"Only when the floor is worthy," she teased.

His mouth curved. "Then perhaps one day, we shall see if Jerusalem's stones are strong enough to bear you."

Makeda sipped her wine, her eyes gleaming. "Stones may bear me, Solomon, but can kings?"

The courtiers around them laughed nervously at the daring words, but the king only smiled more broadly, lifting his goblet in salute. Their eyes met over the rims of their cups, and though the hall was alive with music and feasting, the space between them was a taut, invisible thread.

Servants brought bowls of sweetmeats and pitchers of cool water; the sound of pouring seemed louder than it should have. Makeda felt the pull of his gaze as she reached for her wine instead, refusing the water, though her throat was dry. A choice, small and defiant.

He noticed. Oh, he noticed.

The banquet surged around them—laughter, dancers, music—but beneath it all ran the steady current of two sovereigns circling each other, clever words their weapons, stolen touches their spoils, the promise of something more dangerous always just beyond reach.

Chapter Eighteen

The Pact of Nothing

The palace had quieted after the banquet, its torches burning low, its corridors hushed except for the soft pad of sandals and the distant trickle of fountains.

Makeda stood upon the terrace of her chambers, the night air cool against her skin, the scent of jasmine clinging to her hair. Below, the city slept, its lamps dwindling one by one like fallen stars. She was content to watch in silence—until she felt him.

Solomon did not announce himself. He stepped from the shadow of the archway, a simple cloak over his shoulders, no crown upon his brow. Only the faint gleam of a smile betrayed the king from the man.

"You walk your palace like a thief," Makeda said softly, though her heart had quickened at his nearness.

He came to stand beside her, leaning against the stone rail. "I walk it like a host who does not wish his guest to feel alone."

Her lips curved faintly. "Your hostly duties are tireless, my lord. Are you never weary?"

"Only of easy company," he replied, his eyes glinting. "But yours, Queen of Sheba, is not easy."

For a moment they stood in silence, the wind stirring her robe. At last she said, "You give me riddles by day and banquets by night. Will you now give me treasures as well? Is this how Israel secures alliances—drown a queen in gold until she yields?"

He turned then, studying her face in the torchlight. "I would give you treasures, yes. Gold, silver, rare woods, spices. Whatever your heart desires."

Makeda lifted her chin. "My heart desires nothing from your hand. Sheba is not poor. I will return to my people as I came—rich in my own right."

His smile deepened, slow and deliberate. "Nothing?"

"Nothing," she said firmly.

Solomon straightened, folding his arms across his chest. "Then let us bind it as an oath. You shall take nothing from my house—not jewel, not spice, not garment..." His eyes lingered a moment too long on her lips. "...not even a drop of water."

The words fell into the night like a stone into still water.

Makeda stilled, her pulse beating sharp in her throat. The challenge was spoken lightly, yet it cut deep. She knew the danger of oaths, the weight of words. Still, pride braced her spine.

"So be it," she said, her voice calm though her chest tightened. "I will take nothing."

Their eyes locked, and in that gaze was the spark of battle and the pull of something more perilous. For the first time, she felt that she had not only crossed deserts and rivers, but entered a riddle she might not solve.

Solomon inclined his head slightly, as if satisfied. "Then it is sealed."

And with a smile that was half triumph, half promise, he left her in the torchlit silence of her terrace—alone, except for the echo of his words and the unsettling knowledge that she had agreed to a game she did not yet understand.

Chapter Nineteen

Whispers in the Chamber

The queen's chambers glowed with lamplight, their carved cedar walls perfumed by burning myrrh. Cushions of scarlet and ivory were strewn across the floor, alabaster jars uncorked so that the air grew heavy with rose, cassia, and frankincense. Outside, her guards stood silent, but within the room was a hive of soft hands, silk whispers, and the hush of women tending their queen.

Makeda reclined against bolsters, her eyes half closed as one girl combed her curls, weaving jasmine blossoms through the glistening strands. Another smoothed fragrant oil along the length of her arm until her skin shone. A third knelt at her feet, massaging her calves with scented balm, her fingers reverent in their touch.

It was luxury worthy of a queen, and yet the women's chatter buzzed just beneath the hush.

"Did you see how he looked at her during the feast?" one whispered behind her hand "Not at her," another corrected with a sly grin. "Through her. As though the rest of us did not exist." "He has never watched so before. Not even his favorites," a younger attendant said, her voice half in awe, half in envy.

Makeda's lips curved faintly. She did not open her eyes, but her voice carried clear. "If you whisper of me, at least speak boldly. Queens have no patience for secrets in corners."

The attendants gasped softly, then broke into laughter, emboldened. The youngest leaned closer, mischief in her tone. "Then we say it plainly, Majesty: the king desires you. And you, perhaps, do not despise it."

Makeda opened her eyes then, their dark fire steady. "Desire is no crown. I was not raised to be a prize to please another's longing."

The eldest, wiser than the rest, bowed her head as she rubbed fragrant balm into the queen's hands. "No, Majesty. But even the strongest throne does not shield a woman's heart from being stirred."

The others tittered, emboldened again. "He will not rest, Majesty. He will find a way. He is a hunter, and you are—" one girl stopped, then finished in a whisper—"the prey he has never caught."

Makeda sat straighter, the pearls at her throat gleaming against her skin. "Prey? No. If he hunts, let him find that queens are not beasts of the field. I am sovereign. I yield to no man's chase."

The bold girl lowered her gaze, chastened, though her lips still trembled with a smile. The others hushed, yet their eyes shone with secret delight as they fanned and anointed her, as though tending not merely a queen but a mystery unfolding before them.

When at last the women withdrew, Makeda rose alone. The chamber seemed larger in their absence, the perfume heavier, the silence sharper. She crossed to the bronze mirror set within an ivory frame, the lamplight gilding her reflection.

She studied herself with an unflinching gaze. Her skin gleamed, flawless and intoxicating, her lips full, her lashes long and soft as whispers. Her figure was tall and elegant, curved yet commanding, as though strength itself had been sculpted into feminine form. She was sovereign, radiant, untouchable.

And yet...

Her gaze lingered on her own eyes. In their depths she saw shadows of last night: Solomon leaning too near in the garden, his voice a low snare of words. The memory of his question—*Not even a drop?*—coiled in her chest like smoke.

Her hand drifted to the silver ewer set upon a table, the vessel sweating in the lamplight. She reached as if to pour, then stopped, her fingers hovering above the cool curve of its handle. A simple drink—yet she felt as though the weight of nations balanced on it.

Makeda drew back quickly, unsettled, pressing her palm against the lotus amulet at her throat. *Nothing,* she reminded herself, the word her shield. *I will take nothing.*

But as she looked again into the mirror, her lips curved faintly, betraying a thought she dared not speak aloud: that she was not only sovereign and wise, but a woman, and even queens could thirst.

Chapter Twenty

The Contest Renewed

B y decree of the king, the throne room was filled again. Nobles crowded the marble floor, scribes poised with their reeds, and from the galleries above the women of the harem leaned forward like curious birds, eager for the day's duel.

Makeda entered with the stride of a sovereign, her guard at her back, her jewels gleaming in the sunlight that poured through the high windows. Solomon rose as she approached, bowing just deeply enough to acknowledge her station before reclaiming his throne.

The air was charged. The whole court knew what had been spoken between them the night before—word traveled like fire in dry grass. *She would take nothing. Not gold, not spice... not even a drop of water.* Some whispered that it was clever of her, to bind herself with so proud a vow. Others whispered that it was dangerous, for the king was as cunning as he was wise.

Makeda knew they whispered, and so did Solomon. And perhaps that was why his first words cut straight to the matter.

"Queen of Sheba," he said, his voice carrying through the hall, "you came to test me with hard questions. Yet in your boldness, you have set yourself a harder riddle than any you might pose."

Her chin lifted. "And what riddle is that, my lord?"

"That you will leave Jerusalem with nothing," Solomon replied, a smile playing at his lips. "Not jewel, not spice, not garment—" here his gaze lingered a heartbeat too long "—not even a drop of water. Do you mean to go without feasting, without wine, without a single gift for your people? The world will say Israel has sent Sheba away empty-handed."

A ripple of murmurs passed through the court. Makeda's pulse quickened, but she did not flinch. "The world will say Sheba's queen is rich enough to stand without Israel's gifts," she answered. "What is a treasure gained from another hand? I will take nothing because I have need of nothing."

The chamber hushed. Even the harem women leaned closer, breathless with the audacity of her reply.

Solomon studied her, his dark eyes glinting with something between admiration and challenge. "Very well," he said at last. "Let us see, then, if wisdom and pride weigh more heavily than hunger and thirst."

The tension broke as he gestured to the heralds. The riddles began anew, sharp and dazzling, echoing off the marble pillars.

Makeda answered boldly, her voice smooth, her wit honed. She spoke of love and loss, of justice and betrayal, of treasures greater than gold. Solomon pressed her with riddles of time, of desire, of truth hidden beneath lies. The court gasped and applauded, their duel a dance of minds as dangerous as any clash of swords.

And though the feast went on—goblets poured, platters laden—Makeda lifted only the wine, never the water. She would not forget the weight of her oath.

But as the riddles grew deeper, her throat tightened with thirst. And each time the servants passed with their silver ewers, she felt Solomon's gaze upon her, as though he could already see the moment when pride would bow to desire, and her vow would be broken.

Chapter Twenty-One

Fire in the Court

T he throne room glittered like a jewel, the crowd pressing forward as if each riddle might crack open a secret of heaven itself. Courtiers leaned on carved pillars, scribes bent over their tablets, and from above the women of the harem whispered and laughed, bracelets clinking like tiny bells.

Solomon reclined on his throne, one elbow on the carved lion's arm, his dark gaze never leaving Makeda. She stood across from him, tall and radiant, her light robe flowing with each breath of air.

"Another," Solomon said, his tone deceptively mild. "Tell me, Queen of Sheba—what fire cannot be quenched by water, nor consumed by years, nor buried by earth?"

Makeda lifted her chin, her lashes lowering just enough to veil her eyes. "Desire," she said. "It burns in the hearts of kings and beggars alike, and not even death steals its last ember."

The court murmured, stirred by her boldness. Solomon's smile deepened, slow as a blade drawn from its sheath.

"Well answered," he said. "Then hear this: *What treasure grows greater when given away, yet vanishes when hoarded?*"

Makeda did not hesitate. "Love," she replied, her voice carrying clear through the hall. "Keep it only for yourself and it rots; give it, and it multiplies."

Gasps and nods rippled through the court. Some whispered that her words echoed their own Scriptures, though none dared say so too loudly.

Solomon leaned forward now, his eyes glinting. "And what, Queen of Sheba, is more dangerous than a sword, yet softer than silk?"

Makeda allowed herself a slow smile. She did not answer at once. Instead, she walked forward a pace, the folds of her gown whispering across the marble floor. When she spoke, her voice was low, intimate, yet loud enough to reach every ear.

"A woman's tongue," she said. "It can wound more deeply than iron, yet caress as gently as a feather."

The hall erupted—gasps, laughter, shocked applause. Even the harem above could not contain their giggles. Solomon laughed, rich and warm, though his eyes never left hers.

"Dangerous indeed," he said, his voice edged with admiration. "And if her tongue is matched by her mind, what man can withstand her?"

Makeda's smile turned sharp. "No man need withstand her—if he is wise enough to stand with her."

For a moment the chamber went utterly still, as though the very air bent toward them. The courtiers shifted uneasily, sensing they witnessed not just a game of riddles but a battle of equals, sovereign against sovereign, fire meeting fire.

At last Solomon leaned back, lifting his goblet. "Then to wisdom shared," he said, his voice smooth but his gaze burning.

Makeda lifted her own cup. "And to fire that does not consume, but refines."

They drank, and the hall roared its approval, but every whisper, every glance, carried the same truth: the duel was no longer mere sport. It was a courtship of minds, dangerous and irresistible.

Chapter Twenty-Two

The Last Riddle

The court had grown accustomed to the rhythm of their contests: her riddles like jeweled daggers, his answers quick and gleaming; his questions like nets cast wide, her replies slipping free. Each day the crowds pressed closer, scribes inked faster, and the harem women leaned farther over their lattices, delighting in the spectacle.

But today, the air was different. Whispers wound through the hall before Makeda even entered: her time in Jerusalem was nearing its end. Sheba's throne waited. Her caravans, already heavy with gifts and guards, could not tarry forever.

Makeda entered in wearing gold and saffron, regal as the morning sun, her guard at her back. Solomon stood to greet her, and though his smile was the same, his eyes burned with a sharper light. Today, there would be an ending.

"Queen of Sheba," he said, his voice rich, carrying to every corner of the room, "for many days we have tested each other's wisdom. Let us see, before you depart, which of us will end the contest with the sharper edge."

Makeda's lips curved. "Be warned, my lord. I have yet to be outmatched."

The hall stilled. Solomon leaned forward, his voice dropping into the kind of question that was no riddle at all, yet pierced sharper than any.

"Tell me then, Makeda—what is the one thing a sovereign may not refuse, no matter how proud, no matter how wise?"

Makeda's smile faltered for the first time. She frowned, thinking. Around them, the court held its breath.

"A sovereign may refuse gold," she said slowly. "He may refuse tribute, alliance, even war. But he cannot refuse... his people."

Solomon's smile deepened. "And if the people's demand is thirst?" His hand flicked, and servants poured clear water into silver goblets, the sound bright and cruel in the silence.

Makeda's heart thudded once, sharp. The court gasped at the daring, some laughing nervously, others staring wide-eyed. The oath she had spoken—*not even a drop of water*—was no longer private. It was weapon and theater both.

Her pride rose, sharp as a blade. She lifted her chin, her voice steady though her throat ached dry. "Then Sheba will show the world that thirst itself can be mastered. I will take nothing."

The court erupted—some in admiration, some in disbelief. Solomon only smiled, lifting his own goblet to drink slowly, his eyes never leaving hers.

The tension held, taut as a bowstring, until Solomon set the cup aside. "Then Jerusalem will watch, and Sheba will teach us whether pride is stronger than thirst."

Makeda bowed her head slightly, acknowledging the challenge. "And when I return to my people," she said, her tone cool, regal, "they will know their queen was not undone by any king."

The chamber roared with applause, the courtiers rising to their feet, the scribes scribbling furiously. The duel was done for the day, but its flame was not extinguished. For now, it burned hotter than ever—fanned by the knowledge that her days in Jerusalem were numbered, and the riddle of water remained unsolved.

Chapter Twenty-Three

The Queen's Vigil

The night pressed heavy over Jerusalem, the palace wrapped in silence save for the distant calls of watchmen and the sigh of wind through cedar beams.

Makeda lay awake on her couch of ivory and linen, her attendants dismissed, her chamber hushed but for the faint trickle of a fountain beyond the lattice. The scent of rose oil lingered on her skin, jasmine still curled in her hair, yet sleep would not come.

The contest of the day replayed in her mind—his voice low and sure, his eyes glinting as the servants poured water into silver goblets, the entire court waiting for her to falter. She had not. She had stood firm, her oath unbroken. But her throat had burned, and each swallow of wine had felt heavier than stone.

Not even a drop of water.

She pressed her palm against the lotus amulet at her throat, grounding herself in its cool weight. *I am queen. I will not yield.*

Yet her thoughts would not be stilled. They drifted back across deserts and rivers, to the shaded halls of her father's palace. She remembered crouching behind the carved screens, listening to men argue, her father's hand resting upon her head when the chamber emptied. *Wisdom is the only treasure that cannot be taken from you,* he had said. *Guard it, my daughter. Guard it, and no man will ever master you.*

And yet here, in Jerusalem, she felt the edge of mastery pressing close—not with swords or chains, but with riddles, glances, and a vow she had spoken in pride.

She rose, restless, pacing across the mosaic floor. The lamplight gleamed against the alabaster jars, against the mirror of polished bronze, against the silver ewer set upon the table. Beads of moisture slid down its curve, cool and perfect, catching the glow like liquid jewels.

Makeda stopped, staring at it. Her throat tightened. She stepped closer, drawn, her hand lifting before she knew it. Her fingers hovered above the handle, trembling with the nearness of relief. One sip. One sip, and the burn would vanish.

She snatched her hand back, her breath sharp.

"No," she whispered aloud, her voice firm, as though she addressed her own weakness. "I will not."

She turned from the ewer, but the thought lingered, teasing, relentless. Her mind conjured images of rivers flashing in sunlight, of wells drawn fresh at dawn, of cool water pressed to her lips by hands not her own.

She pressed her hands against her eyes, furious with herself. This was not who she was. She was Makeda, sovereign of Sheba, daughter of kings. No vow, no king, no thirst could unmake her.

And yet, when she lay down once more, she dreamed of water.

It shimmered in bowls of silver, it cascaded from stone fountains, it beaded upon Solomon's fingertips as he offered her a cup. She reached for it even as she whispered *nothing, nothing, nothing.* But the word slipped into the current, carried away, until it was swallowed in the rushing stream.

Makeda woke with a start, her skin damp, her lips dry, her heart hammering in her chest. The fountain outside whispered on, merciless, reminding her that the hardest riddle she had ever faced was not one she could speak aloud, but one she had bound upon herself.

Chapter Twenty-Four

The Water and the Flame

The moon rode high, casting silver across the courtyards, the gardens, the still pools of Solomon's palace. In her chamber, Makeda dismissed her women at last, craving solitude. They withdrew with bows and whispers, leaving her with only the murmur of a fountain beyond the lattice and the shimmer of lamplight on polished walls.

Upon the table sat a silver ewer, beaded with droplets that caught the light like stars. Beside it, a goblet gleamed, empty.

Makeda gazed at it for a long while, her hands folded tightly at her waist. The oath rang in her mind: *I will take nothing. Not even a drop of water.* She had said it boldly, and all Jerusalem had heard. Yet here she stood, her heart restless with the weight of her vow.

At last she turned to her guard. "Summon the king."

Moments later Solomon entered, cloaked in shadow, no crown upon his brow, but no less king. His broad shoulders filled the doorway, his bearing powerful even in simple robes. His eyes found hers at once, steady and intent, glinting in the lamplight.

"You called for me," he said, his voice low, resonant, a voice that seemed to stir the air itself.

Makeda inclined her head, her composure unshaken. "Yes. Because I will not let whispers say I was caught in a snare unawares. If I break my vow, it will be before your eyes, and it will be by my choosing."

Something flickered across his face—admiration, hunger, triumph. "Then Sheba's queen is not only wise," he murmured, stepping closer, "but brave enough to admit her pride."

Makeda lifted the goblet and poured. The water flowed smooth and silver, the sound loud in the silence. She raised it, her eyes locked with his.

"I made an oath in pride," she said, her voice steady. "But wisdom is not to cling to pride until it shatters us. Tonight I choose differently."

She brought her lips slowly to the goblet and she drank. One slow, deliberate sip. The water gleamed on her lips as she lowered the cup.

A breath left Solomon, rougher than before. He closed the distance between them in a single stride, his presence overwhelming—heat, cedar, wine. His gaze swept her face, lingering on her mouth, before rising to her eyes with an intensity that made her pulse quicken.

"You have taken," he said, his voice husky now. "Not gold, not spice, not garment... but water."

Makeda's chin lifted, though her breath betrayed her. "Yes. And in taking, I have answered the last riddle."

He reached for her then, his hand strong as it enclosed hers, the other rising to cup her cheek. His thumb traced the curve of her jaw, reverent yet possessive, and she shivered at his touch. His nearness was intoxicating—the breadth of his chest against her, the heat of his breath brushing her lips, the firmness of his body telling her beyond words that he wanted her.

Her lips parted, and he claimed them. The kiss was not tentative—it was sure, deep, hungry, as though every riddle and duel had led him to this moment. He tasted of wine and spice, of power and promise. His hand slid to the curve of her waist, drawing her closer, until she felt herself molded against the strength of him, her pulse answering the thrum of his.

Makeda's arms rose, fingers curling into his hair, marveling at its softness. He groaned low in his throat at her touch, a sound that thrilled her to the core. When he deepened the kiss, his lips moving with slow mastery, she felt her resolve melt into something richer, more dangerous: desire unguarded.

The fountain whispered beyond the lattice, the water a witness to her surrender and his triumph. Yet in this union there was no conquest, no defeat. Pride had been set aside, and in its place was fire—two sovereigns equal at last, bound not by crown or oath, but by longing.

When at last they parted, his forehead rested against hers, his hand still cradling her cheek, his breath uneven. His eyes burned into hers with a tenderness fierce enough to shake her.

"So this is how riddles end?" she whispered.

His lips curved, brushing hers once more. "No, Makeda. This is how they begin."

Chapter Twenty-Five

Morning in Jerusalem

The first light of dawn brushed the city, gilding the stones of Jerusalem in pale gold. The palace stirred with the rustle of servants and the calls of watchmen changing guard, but within the queen's chambers it was still.

Makeda sat upon the cushioned bench by the lattice window, her hair loose about her shoulders, a linen robe draped across her. The faint scent of cedar clung to her skin, mingled with jasmine and wine. She touched the silver goblet upon the table—the one from the night before—and for the first time since her vow she smiled at it without unease.

Behind her the chamber remained hushed, yet she felt his presence still, as if the warmth of his hands lingered on her skin. She remembered the way he had looked at her afterward—eyes softened, voice low—as they lay in the quiet after desire's fire had ebbed.

"Makeda," he had whispered, her name shaped like a secret. "You are not prize nor conquest. You are the riddle God himself set before me—and the answer I did not know I sought."

Even now, recalling it, her heart gave a small, traitorous ache. For she had come to test him, to measure wisdom against wisdom, and instead she had found something far more dangerous.

Outside, the corridors hummed. She heard the footsteps of courtiers, the laughter of concubines drifting from their galleries. No doubt tongues already wagged. They would say the queen had yielded, that the wise king had ensnared her. Let them. Makeda knew the truth—that she had chosen, and in choosing, she had met him as equal.

She rose, drawing the robe more firmly about her shoulders. Her reflection in the bronze mirror showed her not diminished but radiant, her eyes brighter, her bearing more assured. She was no less queen than she had been the day before. If anything, she carried herself with a new, quiet fire.

Soon she would depart. Her throne waited in Sheba, her people expecting her return. Yet she knew that when she crossed the deserts again, she would not carry only gifts and stories. She would carry the memory of the night Solomon had spoken to her not as king to queen, but as man to woman—and how she, sovereign of Sheba, had answered not with words but with the truth of her own heart.

Makeda turned from the window as the first rays of sunlight spilled into the chamber. A new day had come, and with it, the knowledge that her time in Jerusalem was drawing to its end.

But even as she stepped into the brightness, she knew the flame kindled between them would not be easily extinguished.

Chapter Twenty-Six

The Temple of the Lord

The morning was bright, the sky a flawless blue above Jerusalem. Makeda had seen the terraces and the palaces, the halls of cedar, the courts lined with gold. Yet as Solomon stood beside her upon the terrace, he smiled—not the smile of a king boasting of riches, but of a man eager to share what he treasured most.

"You have seen my house," he said, his eyes glinting with reverence, "but not the house of the One who gave me all. Come, Makeda. Walk with me, and I will show you the Temple of the Lord—the dwelling place of the living God. He is not like the gods carved of wood or hammered from stone, silent and blind. Here the Lord speaks to His people, and His presence fills the air itself. If anything in Jerusalem is worthy of your journey, it is this."

He extended his hand—not command, but invitation.

Makeda hesitated, her heart stirring. She had heard tales whispered by merchants and travelers—of the God of Israel who had split seas, who had fed His people with bread from heaven, who had crushed mighty kings and lifted shepherd boys onto thrones. Were they tales or truths? She did not know. And yet, it was in her nature to test, to see beneath words, to measure stories against reality. Just as she unraveled riddles, she must know for herself.

At last, she placed her fingers lightly in his. "Then show me," she said, her voice low but steady. "Let me see if what I have heard is legend or truth." She donned a veil covering her hair and went with him.

Their eyes met, and for a moment neither spoke. After the night they had shared, there was no hiding what lay between them. His gaze lingered on her face with warmth and gravity, not only the desire of a man but the respect of one who had found his equal. She returned the look, her chin lifted, her lips soft with the memory of his kiss. What they had discovered in one another was fire, yes—but now there was something else waiting, deeper than passion.

Together they descended toward the courts where the Temple rose, gleaming in the sun.

The white stones blazed with brilliance, the gilded doors glimmered like fire. The bronze pillars Jachin and Boaz stood at the entrance, towering, immovable, their names meaning "He will establish" and "In Him is strength." Smoke from the altar curled upward in a fragrant column, carrying the scent of sacrifice toward heaven.

Makeda slowed, the weight of the place pressing upon her. She had walked through shrines in Egypt, temples in Sheba, sanctuaries filled with idols of stone and wood. They had dazzled with splendor, yes—but this was different. This place was alive with something unseen, a presence that seemed to draw breath itself.

Solomon walked at her side, not as king displaying wealth, but as priest-king, his face solemn, reverent. "This is the house of the Lord," he said softly. "Not built by my wisdom, but by His command. All that I have—all wealth, all wisdom, all glory—was granted because I asked not for riches nor long life, but for understanding to govern His people. And He, in His mercy, gave more than I sought."

Makeda looked at him then, and for the first time she did not see only the man, or the king, or the lover whose touch still lingered in her memory. She saw the servant of a God greater than any she had known.

They entered the inner court. Priests in white garments moved in silence, their faces solemn. Golden lampstands cast steady flames, the table of showbread gleamed with loaves, and before the curtain that hid the Most Holy Place, incense rose in a veil of smoke.

Makeda's breath caught. Her skin prickled with awe. Here was no idol shaped by hands, no silent effigy. Here was the unseen, the holy, the living God who had chosen Israel for His dwelling.

Solomon turned to her, his voice low but firm. "You came to test me with riddles. You came to see if the tales of my wisdom were true. But Makeda—" his eyes burned with quiet intensity—"this is the source. Not my mind, not my hand, not my throne. All flows from the Lord who dwells here."

She pressed her hand to her heart, steadying herself. Pride had carried her across deserts. Desire had drawn her into his arms. But now something deeper moved within her: conviction, reverence, a flame that would not be quenched.

Makeda felt the heavy presence of God in this place, unlike anything she had ever experienced. She sank to her knees upon the cold stone floor, declaring "Blessed be the Lord your God, who has delighted in you and set you on the throne of Israel. For truly there is no God like Him in all the earth."

The court fell silent, every eye fixed upon the foreign queen kneeling in Israel's Temple.

Solomon's hand came to rest gently upon her shoulder—not as king to subject, but as man to woman, as servant to seeker. His voice was quiet, yet it carried to every corner of the holy place. "And now, Makeda, queen of Sheba, you have found the answer to the greatest riddle of all."

She lifted her eyes, shimmering with emotion, and in that moment she knew: her journey had not been for wealth or wisdom alone, nor even for the fire of desire. It had been to find this God, the One who had granted Solomon all things.

And destiny itself shifted beneath her feet.

Chapter Twenty-Seven

Reflections in Her Chamber

The palace quieted with the fall of night. Torches flickered in the corridors, and the murmur of the city faded into stillness. In her chamber, Makeda reclined upon cushions, her women gathered close, braiding threads of gold into her robe for the morning's court. The scent of myrrh hung in the air, warm and sweet.

Yet her thoughts were far from the silks and perfumes.

She had stood within the Temple of the Lord, her knees upon the cold stone floor, and for the first time in her life she had felt herself small before something greater than crown, greater than nation. Not fear, but awe. Not dread, but the startling weight of truth.

Her women glanced at her often, whispering to one another when they thought she did not hear. One, bold enough to speak, set down her ivory comb and said, "My queen, you shine tonight. But it is not the lamps that make you radiant. Tell us, what stirs in your heart?"

Makeda smiled faintly. "You saw it too, then."

"We saw you kneel," the young woman said softly. "And we saw his eyes upon you. It seemed as though king and queen were not alone in that place."

Makeda's hand drifted to the lotus amulet at her throat. "Not alone," she murmured. "I have seen gods carved of stone, gods gilded in gold, gods worshiped in silence. But in this Temple..." She drew a breath. "In this Temple, I felt a God who listens. A God who answers. A God who gives wisdom and breathes life."

The women fell silent, struck by her tone.

Makeda turned her gaze toward the open lattice where the stars shimmered above Jerusalem. "I came here seeking riddles, eager to test the wisdom of a king. But what I found is that his wisdom is not his own. It is gift. It is flame lent from heaven. And I... I am humbled by it."

Her women exchanged glances, some uneasy, some moved. To hear their queen speak of humility was no small thing.

Makeda leaned back, her expression unreadable yet softened by an inner fire. She thought of Solomon's face in the Temple, solemn and reverent, and of his face in the shadows of her chamber, tender and near. Desire had bound them for a night, but something deeper tied her heart now—something she could not yet name.

And yet, time pressed upon her. The throne of Sheba awaited her return. Her people needed their queen. She could not linger forever in Jerusalem, no matter how the thought of leaving twisted inside her.

She rose, dismissing her women with a graceful wave of her hand. Alone at last, she whispered into the silence, "Perhaps this, too, is a riddle. Not how a queen might win a king, but how two sovereigns, touched by the same God, might walk separate paths and yet remain bound by destiny."

The stars outside seemed to shimmer in answer.

Chapter Twenty-Eight

The Farewell Banquet

The banquet hall blazed with light. Hundreds of oil lamps flickered against carved cedar beams, their flames mirrored in bowls of polished bronze and in the jeweled eyes of golden lions flanking the dais. Musicians filled the air with the hum of lyres and the pulse of tambourines, while dancers swirled in bright silks. The scent of roasted lamb, honey cakes, and wine steeped with spices filled the air.

Makeda entered at Solomon's side, light as a whisper transparent golden sleeves flowing behind her like banners. Her guard followed at a respectful distance, but it was not spears or silks that drew every gaze. It was her bearing—calm, radiant, sovereign. The queen of Sheba walked as one who had tested the heart of a king and found it true.

At the high table, Solomon raised his goblet, his voice carrying over the noise. "This night we honor Makeda, daughter of kings, sovereign of Sheba, whose wisdom is as sharp as her beauty, and whose journey has brought honor to Jerusalem."

The court roared its approval, goblets lifted, spears striking the stone floor.

Servants entered in procession, bearing treasures: caskets of gold, carved ivory, bolts of royal cloth, alabaster jars of incense, heaps of gems that glittered like captured stars. They were laid before Makeda until the dais itself seemed a mountain of wealth.

"Take them," Solomon said, his eyes never leaving hers. "Gifts for a queen worthy of all kingdoms, so that Sheba may know how dearly Jerusalem esteems her."

A murmur rippled through the court—admiration, envy, awe.

But Makeda's lips curved in a smile both gracious and defiant. She rose, her voice carrying clear as a bell: "I have seen your riches, Solomon, and I have seen your wisdom. And I tell you this—no gold, no jewel, no perfume can compare with what I have already taken from Jerusalem."

The hall stirred, whispers darting like sparks. The courtiers leaned forward, wondering.

Solomon's eyes gleamed, his smile slow, knowing. "Ah," he said softly, though his words reached every corner of the room, "but tell me, Queen of Sheba—what is it you have taken?"

Makeda inclined her head, her long hair brushing her shoulders, her eyes glimmering with secret fire. "A drink of water," she said. "And with it, a wisdom I will carry home to my people."

The court erupted—some gasping, some laughing, some startled into silence. To many it seemed a jest, but those nearest the dais caught the double edge in her tone. Solomon's gaze lingered on her a moment longer, heat and reverence mingled, before he lifted his goblet in salute.

"Then Sheba has chosen well," he said, and drank deeply.

The banquet surged on—music swelling, dancers leaping, laughter echoing through the hall. But beneath it all ran the silent current between king and queen, words wrapped in riddles, glances heavy with memory. And though the court feasted on lamb and honey, they feasted on each other's company, knowing the taste of parting was near.

Chapter Twenty-Nine

The Garden Farewell

After the banquet's clamor had faded into music and laughter behind the palace doors, Solomon led Makeda into the hush of his garden. The night air was cool, fragrant with myrtle and pomegranate blossoms. Moonlight draped the marble paths in silver, and the pools mirrored stars as though heaven itself had stooped to gaze.

They walked in silence for a time, her hand resting lightly upon his arm, their steps slow, reluctant. The distant strains of music reached them like echoes from another world, but here, among the shadowed trees, there was only the two of them.

At last Solomon spoke. "Jerusalem will wake tomorrow knowing the Queen of Sheba prepares to depart. And I... I must learn how to walk these courts without your shadow beside mine."

Makeda's lips curved faintly, though her eyes glistened. "And I must cross the desert knowing the sound of your voice will not follow me. A queen cannot dwell forever in another's palace, no matter how splendid."

He turned toward her then, catching her hand in his. His thumb brushed over her fingers, slow, reverent. "No, a queen cannot. But you are not only queen to me, Makeda. You are riddle and fire, wisdom and beauty, the answer to prayers I did not know I prayed."

Her breath caught. She lowered her gaze, lashes sweeping shadows upon her cheeks. "And you, Solomon—you are the question I never knew I was seeking. I will carry the memory of you, as surely as I carry the faith of the God I found in your Temple."

He drew her close, his forehead resting lightly against hers. The warmth of him, the strength of his frame, the scent of cedar that clung to his robes—all pressed into her senses, carving the moment deep into memory.

Their lips met, lingering, unhurried. Not the hungry fire of that first night, but something steadier, weighted with longing and farewell. A kiss not of conquest, but of remembrance.

When they parted, Solomon searched her face as though memorizing every line. "If destiny is kind," he whispered, "our paths will cross again."

Makeda's smile trembled, half pride, half sorrow. "And if it is not... then let this be enough."

A silence fell, broken only by the sigh of wind through the leaves. They stood there a moment longer, two sovereigns bound by something both fragile and eternal, knowing that dawn would part them.

At last, she stepped back, her hand slipping from his. Her eyes shone like dark jewels in the moonlight. "Farewell, Solomon."

"Farewell, Makeda."

She turned and walked into the shadows of the garden, her veils whispering against the marble. Solomon watched until she vanished from sight, the night air heavy with the ache of love and the weight of destiny.

Chapter Thirty

Return to Sheba

The city of Jerusalem dwindled behind them, its golden rooftops and shining Temple fading into the haze of morning light. Makeda's caravan stretched like a jeweled serpent across the hills: camels swaying beneath loads of incense and ivory, guards marching with spears that caught the sun, handmaidens veiled against the dust.

The people of Jerusalem had lined the walls to watch her depart, their cheers echoing across the valleys. But now the desert wind claimed her, hot and dry, carrying only the creak of saddles and the rhythmic thud of hooves.

Makeda rode high upon her litter draped in crimson, her head lifted toward the horizon. Yet her gaze was not fixed on the sands before her. Inwardly, her thoughts lingered in the shadowed garden, in the glow of the Temple, in the press of Solomon's hand against hers.

She pressed her palm lightly against her breast where the lotus amulet rested. *I came for riddles,* she thought. *I leave with answers I never sought.*

Around her, her women whispered as they fanned her, some speaking in wonder of the feasts and splendor they had seen, others gossiping still about the king's eyes upon their mistress. Makeda listened in silence, but within her a deeper current stirred.

She had come to measure the wisdom of a man, and she had found it. But more—she had found the source of that wisdom. The memory of the Temple clung to her as firmly as Solomon's touch. She had seen priests lifting their hands, had smelled the incense rising like a prayer, had felt a Presence greater than kings. She had bowed, not to Solomon, but to the God who had chosen him.

The desert stretched ahead, vast and merciless, yet she did not feel bereft. She carried something invisible but eternal. A flame lit in Jerusalem now burned within her, one that no distance could dim.

Still, when the night winds cooled and the caravan made camp beneath the stars, her heart ached. She would sit apart from her women, her gaze lifted to the heavens, wondering if Solomon too looked upward at that same hour. If he thought of her. If the bond they had forged would endure across deserts and kingdoms.

A queen cannot dwell forever in another's palace. She must return to her people, her throne, her duties. Yet Makeda knew that her life's path had bent upon this journey, that her story would never again be only her own. Destiny had shifted beneath her feet in Jerusalem, and though she could not name it yet, she felt its weight with every step of her return.

Chapter Thirty-One

Queen of Sheba Returned

The gates of Marib opened wide, and the people of Sheba poured into the streets to welcome their queen. Drums thundered, incense curled into the sky, and palm branches lined her path. The long desert journey was forgotten in the surge of joy that swept through the city at her return.

Makeda descended from her litter with regal grace, her guard forming a proud wall of steel behind her. The treasures of Jerusalem followed in procession—gems, ivory, and silks—but it was not the gold that drew her people's awe. It was their queen herself.

They whispered of her radiance. Her skin gleamed, her eyes bright with a new fire, her bearing more assured than ever. Some said she walked taller, as if touched by the hand of heaven. Mothers lifted children high to see her, elders bowed low, and in every gaze there was both love and wonder.

In the days that followed, she took her throne again, but her rule was not as it had been before. The court noticed it first: her judgments came swifter, clearer, tempered with mercy. She listened longer before she spoke, yet when she did, her words carried the weight of stone. Merchants found her trade agreements shrewder than before, priests found her questions piercing, and her generals found her counsel keener than steel.

But it was not only her wisdom that stirred her people. It was her words. She spoke of a God unlike their own idols, a God not carved or gilded but living and unseen, who had given Israel's king his brilliance. She told of the Temple that shimmered like a jewel on Mount Zion, where smoke rose not for statues but for the Lord who hears and answers.

Some resisted, muttering that Sheba had gods enough. Others listened with wide eyes, their hearts quickened by her conviction. And through her words, a seed was sown that would outlast her lifetime, a seed that still bore fruit in the generations to come.

At night, in the quiet of her palace, Makeda would walk the colonnades and look to the north. The desert stretched endless between her and Jerusalem, yet she felt it still—the bond forged with the man who had shown her a wisdom greater than his own.

Her people saw only a queen returned in glory. They could not know that beneath her crown, her heart carried something more: the memory of a king's kiss, the echo of a God's voice, and a destiny not yet revealed.

And so the Queen of Sheba reigned, her land flourishing beneath her hand, her story already whispered in markets and sung in caravans. A story that even in far-off lands, even in distant ages, would not be forgotten.

Chapter Thirty-Two

Letters Across the Desert

C aravans still moved between Jerusalem and Sheba, bearing spices southward and gold northward. But now and then, tucked among ivory tusks or jars of incense, there lay a sealed scroll marked with the seal of a lion or a lotus. And those who bore them knew better than to break the wax.

They were letters—his to her, hers to him.

From Solomon to Makeda

To Makeda, queen of Sheba, whose eyes I see even when I close my own:

The halls are quieter without your steps. My courtiers bring petitions, my scribes heap scrolls, my musicians play, but still the air feels wanting. The garden is the same, yet not the same without you.

When I stand in the Temple, I remember your voice lifted there. When I drink water, I remember your lips upon the cup.

I think often of our riddles. Tell me, Makeda—what is the distance between two sovereigns who cannot touch, yet cannot forget? I have not yet found the answer.

—Solomon

From Makeda to Solomon

To Solomon, king of Israel, whose wisdom is sharper than the desert wind:

The desert is long, yet your words find me swiftly. My people rejoiced at my return, yet even in their singing I thought of you.

You ask the distance between two sovereigns who cannot touch, yet cannot forget. I say it is no distance at all. For when I kneel in prayer, I feel your God close, and in that closeness, you are near also.

Do not think me conquered, Solomon. I remain queen of Sheba, and my pride stands tall. But pride has learned a new humility in Jerusalem. And in that, I do not regret one drop of water.

—Makeda

From Solomon

To Makeda, whose words are sweeter than honey from the comb:

You are right. The God who binds the heavens has bound us as well. Perhaps distance is only a riddle with one answer: faith.

Still, I am man as well as king, and I confess, I long for more than faith. I long for your voice, your hand, the way your eyes struck me silent when you smiled. Jerusalem remembers you, Makeda. And so do I.

—Solomon

From Makeda

To Solomon, whose voice lingers though I read only ink:

Your words reach me like cool water in the heat of the day.

I walk my gardens, I sit upon my throne, I judge the disputes of my people. They see their queen radiant, stronger than before, and they rejoice. Yet they cannot know that in the quiet of night, when the torches burn low, I remember the king of Israel who showed me the house of the living God.

And though I do not name it aloud, I feel destiny still shifting beneath my feet.

—Makeda

Thus their letters traveled back and forth, like whispered promises carried by the desert wind. And though kingdoms lay between them, their words bridged the distance, keeping alive both their longing and the flame of faith that had begun in Jerusalem.

Chapter Thirty-Three

The Revelation

The days in Sheba grew longer, and the palace settled into its rhythm once more. Merchants clamored at the gates, generals debated in the council hall, and priests brought incense to their altars. Yet in the quiet hours, Makeda sensed something stirring within her—first a weariness that lingered too long, then a tenderness in her body that no physician's balm could explain.

At first she told no one. She walked the gardens as before, her hand resting lightly at her side, her thoughts turning northward. She remembered Solomon's touch, his kiss, his voice whispering her name in the hush of night. She remembered the Temple's flame, the God who had bound them with wisdom and desire. And slowly, the truth came to her.

Life quickened within her.

When the midwives at last confirmed it, her heart trembled. She sat upon her throne that evening with a new gravity, her hand pressed gently against her womb. A queen of Sheba she had always been, but now—now she was more. She was mother to a child whose bloodline tied two kingdoms together, whose destiny would stretch farther than the deserts between.

Her women wept with joy, bringing garlands and songs. Her council praised heaven for granting their queen an heir. The people rejoiced in the streets, drums echoing beneath the stars.

Yet in the stillness of night, Makeda went alone to her chamber window. She looked northward across the sands, her eyes lifted toward the unseen city of Jerusalem. "Solomon," she whispered, her lips trembling with both longing and wonder. "You are with me still."

She thought of the boy yet unborn, and already she knew his name: **Menelik**—"son of the wise." He would grow with the strength of Sheba and the wisdom of Israel, a living bond between her people and his.

Makeda bowed her head, the weight of destiny pressing upon her as surely as the crown upon her brow. She had gone to Jerusalem seeking riddles. She had returned with the greatest mystery of all—a child who would carry both her heart and Solomon's into the ages.

And so the queen of Sheba smiled, her eyes bright with tears, knowing that her story was not ending, but beginning again in the life stirring within her.

Chapter Thirty-Four

Word Reaches Jerusalem

The court of Israel was in session when the messenger arrived. Dust clung to his robes, his lips parched from the desert, but in his eyes burned urgency. Guards moved to bar his path, but Solomon, seated upon his throne of ivory and gold, lifted his hand.

"Let him speak," the king commanded.

The man fell to his knees, pressing his forehead to the floor. "My lord Solomon, king of Israel, I bring tidings from Sheba."

The hall grew hushed, courtiers leaning forward, scribes pausing their quills. Even the women of the harem, hidden behind their lattices, pressed closer to hear.

Solomon's heart stirred, though his face remained calm. "Rise. Speak what you have been sent to tell."

The messenger lifted his eyes. "Your majesty—the queen has borne an heir."

A murmur swept the court, like wind through a field of grain. Solomon's hand tightened upon the arm of his throne, though his voice remained steady. "An heir?"

The messenger bowed again. "A son, my lord. Strong and well. The people of Sheba rejoice, and they sing his name already: **Menelik.**"

The name struck Solomon's chest like an arrow. Menelik—*son of the wise.* He could not mistake the meaning. His breath caught, his heart fierce with pride, wonder, and an ache he had not allowed himself to feel since she departed.

The court erupted in whispers, counselors trading glances, priests murmuring about prophecy and destiny. But Solomon lifted his hand, silencing them all.

He rose from his throne, his robes sweeping the steps like flowing flame. His eyes, dark with emotion, fixed upon the north. "Blessed be the Lord," he said, his voice carrying strong and clear. "For He has bound Sheba and Israel with blood, as He has already bound them with wisdom."

The scribes hurried to ink his words, the courtiers bowed low, but Solomon stood apart, his thoughts far beyond the chamber. He remembered the night she summoned him, her hand steady as she raised the cup of water. He remembered her voice in the Temple, trembling yet sure: *There is no God like Him in all the earth.*

Now their bond had become flesh and blood.

Solomon turned to Zadok the priest and Benaiah his captain. "Prepare an embassy. Gifts, camels, men of strength and learning. Jerusalem will honor the queen of Sheba and her son, for they are bound to me as to Israel."

The court bowed in assent, the decision sealed. Yet as Solomon returned to his throne, a quiet smile touched his lips. For he knew this was more than politics, more than alliance. It was the work of God, and the unfolding of a riddle whose answer would shape kingdoms.

Chapter Thirty-Five

The King's Journey

The desert stretched wide, its sands shimmering like a sea of gold. Across it moved a company unlike any seen before: Solomon, king of Israel, journeying southward with his captains, his scribes, and a caravan laden with gifts. Ivory gleamed on the pack-camels, bolts of linen caught the sun, and vessels of wine and oil shimmered like jewels. But it was not riches that drew the king into the wilderness. It was love.

He rode at the head, cloaked in white, the lion seal of Judah glinting upon his chest. His gaze never faltered from the horizon, where Sheba waited. The songs of his men rose behind him, but his own heart was quiet, steady with the rhythm of anticipation. He had sent embassies, he had sent word, but now he came himself. For a queen had given him more than riddles or gold. She had given him a son.

When at last the towers of Marib rose in the distance, the desert caravan swelled with the sound of horns. The people of Sheba poured from the gates, marveling at the sight of the king of Israel. Drums pounded, women ululated, garlands of palm were cast along the road.

Makeda stood upon the palace steps, veiled shades of cinnabar, her bearing radiant as ever. Yet when her eyes met Solomon's, the formality of courts and crowns seemed to fall away. Her lips curved, her gaze softened, and for a moment they were not king and queen, but man and woman reunited after too long a parting.

Solomon dismounted, his steps sure upon the stone. He bowed—not low, for no king bows as subject—but deep enough to honor the sovereign who had tested his heart and shared his fire. Makeda inclined her head in return, and when their hands met, the court gasped at the boldness of such closeness.

But the murmur stilled when the queen's nurse approached, carrying a child swaddled in linen. The air hushed as Makeda lifted her son and placed him gently in Solomon's arms.

The king of Israel looked down upon the boy, his breath catching. Menelik's eyes opened wide, and Solomon felt as though the heavens themselves had opened with them. He traced a finger across the child's cheek, marveling at the softness of skin, the tiny fist that closed around his hand.

"My son," he whispered, the words thick with wonder. "Bone of my bone, flesh of my flesh." He looked up at Makeda, his eyes shining. "He is strong. He is ours."

Makeda's smile trembled, fierce and tender at once. "He is the future, Solomon. A bridge between Sheba and Israel."

The people of Sheba lifted their voices in cheers, drums echoing against the palace walls. Yet Solomon heard none of it. In that moment, all sound faded but the quiet breath of the child in his arms, and the steady heartbeat of the woman beside him.

Chapter Thirty-Six

A Final Night

The palace of Marib slept beneath the stars, its walls hushed after the feasting of the day. The torches guttered low, casting long shadows across the courtyards where the fountains murmured softly.

In her chamber, Makeda dismissed her women with a wave of her hand. When the last veil of the door had fallen, Solomon entered, cloaked not in royal robes but in the simplicity of a man seeking only the woman he loved.

For a moment they stood apart, gazing at one another as if to memorize every line, every curve, every breath. She was radiant in silken white, her hair loose upon her shoulders, her skin gleaming softly in the lamplight. He was strong and solemn, his eyes burning with the gravity of a man who knew the night was a gift, not a promise of forever.

Makeda's lips curved in a wry smile. "You cross deserts and kingdoms for one night?"

His voice was low, threaded with warmth. "For one night with you, I would cross them twice over."

She laughed softly, but her eyes glistened. When he reached for her, she did not resist. His hands were strong, reverent as they cupped her face, his thumbs brushing the corners of her mouth as though to memorize her smile. She leaned into his touch, her own hands resting against the breadth of his chest, feeling the steady thrum of his heart.

Their lips met, slow at first, tasting of memory and farewell. The kiss deepened, rich with unspoken words, and she melted into the strength of his embrace. Desire stirred, yes—but beneath it ran something deeper: the certainty that what they shared was not fleeting passion, but the binding of two souls who had touched eternity together.

Later, as they lay entwined upon the cushions, the night breeze cooling their skin, words came softly.

"You changed me," Makeda whispered, her fingers tracing the line of his arm. "I came seeking riddles and found God. I came seeking wisdom and found love."

Solomon pressed a kiss to her temple, his voice low. "And I found in you the mirror of my heart. Not a subject, not a rival, but a sovereign who matched me step for step."

They lay in silence for a time, listening to the fountain's murmur, to the rhythm of each other's breath.

Makeda turned to him at last, her gaze steady. "Tomorrow you must return to your people, and I to mine. We are king and queen before we are man and woman."

He nodded, though his hand tightened around hers. "Yes. But tonight—tonight we are only Solomon and Makeda. And that is enough."

Their lips found each other once more, slow and lingering, sealing not a promise of future, but a remembrance strong enough to last a lifetime.

Chapter Thirty-Seven

The Son of Two Kingdoms

Y ears passed, and the boy grew.

Menelik was quick of mind and strong of limb, his laughter carrying across the palace courtyards like music. The scribes said his questions pierced as sharply as his father's, the captains said he rode a horse as though born to it, and the women of the court whispered that he bore the beauty of both his mother and his father.

When Solomon's envoys came again to Sheba, they bowed before the child as they did before the queen. They brought scrolls of learning, gifts of cedar and fine linen, and words from the king himself: *Raise him in strength and wisdom, for he is mine as well as yours.*

Makeda watched her son chase the wind across the gardens, his curls glinting in the sun, radiant with health. Pride swelled in her chest, yet it was mingled with something deeper, almost aching. For every time she looked upon him, she saw not only her heir but the man who had fathered him—the king of Israel, the lover who had left his mark upon her heart forever.

At night, when the boy slept, she would walk the colonnades and lift her gaze northward. She knew Solomon too thought of their son, though kingdoms kept them apart. Menelik was proof that their bond had not ended with a farewell kiss. He was flesh of their flesh, a bridge between nations, a living riddle whose answer would shape the ages.

The people of Sheba rejoiced, for they saw in their prince the promise of strength and wisdom to come. Yet only Makeda knew the truth in its fullness: that this child was not only heir to her throne, but heir to a love that had defied distance, pride, and even time.

Menelik was the son of two kingdoms—born of a love that destiny itself had written.

Chapter Thirty-Eight

Farewell, Yet Forever

The years had passed, yet their bond had not dimmed. Caravans still moved between Sheba and Israel, bearing gifts, scrolls, and words carried across deserts. But this time, the words were not only of trade or treaty. They were of love—unwritten, unspoken, yet pulsing beneath every line.

And so it was that Solomon came once more to Sheba, not with fanfare of horns or mountains of gold, but quietly, as a man seeking what his heart could not forget.

Makeda met him in the gardens where fountains sang and palms swayed in the night breeze. Time had touched them both, but lightly. His hair was streaked with silver, her eyes held deeper fire, but when their gazes met, it was as though no day had passed since the night of the water and the flame.

They walked together in silence at first, their hands finding each other as naturally as breath. At last Solomon spoke, his voice low, threaded with reverence. "I have had riches, wisdom, power beyond measure. But none of it burns in memory like the moment you lifted that cup to your lips, Makeda. None of it endures like you."

She smiled, her lips soft with longing. "And I, who tested you with riddles, found that the truest answer was not wisdom nor wealth, but love. A love that crossed deserts, a love that bore a son, a love that time itself cannot diminish."

He drew her close, his forehead resting against hers, his hands strong yet tender at her waist. Their kiss lingered, slow and deep, not the fire of discovery but the flame of remembrance, steady and eternal. In that moment, they were not king and queen, not sovereigns weighed with crowns, but Solomon and Makeda—man and woman bound forever.

When they parted, tears shone in her eyes, though her smile remained. "We cannot dwell in the same land," she whispered. "But we dwell in the same destiny. Through our son, through our faith, through what has passed between us—we are tied beyond time."

Solomon's voice was husky with feeling. "Yes. And though kingdoms will rise and fall, though temples will be built and broken, our love will stand in the shadows of history. It will be remembered."

Under the eternal stars they remained, wrapped in a night that seemed to pause for them alone. And when at last they drew apart, no parting words were needed—for theirs was a story written not in sand to be blown away, but in stone, and in blood.

And so it was: Solomon and the Queen of Sheba, bound forever by love, wisdom, and destiny.

Epilogue — The Ark and the Riddle

Years later, stories spread across kingdoms like desert fire: that Menelik, son of Solomon and Makeda, journeyed north to meet his father. That he returned to Ethiopia with wisdom, with treasures, and perhaps with the Ark of the Covenant itself.

Some said it was the true Ark, carried under veil and shadow to rest in Axum, guarded through generations. Others whispered it was but a copy, a riddle woven by Solomon and his son to safeguard the holy relic. And so the mystery endures, carried on the lips of priests and poets, never answered, never silenced.

But beyond the Ark, beyond the riddles, one truth remained: the love between Solomon and Makeda changed the course of nations. Their union was written not in the dust of passing time, but in the stone of history and the blood of a child whose name carried both Israel and Sheba.

And centuries later, when the Son of God Himself walked among men, He remembered her.

"The Queen of the South shall rise up in the judgment with this generation, and shall condemn it: for she came from the uttermost parts of the earth to hear the wisdom of Solomon; and behold, a greater than Solomon is here." — Matthew 12:42

Thus her journey was not only for love, nor even for wisdom, but for eternity.

Letter from the Author

Dear Reader,

The story of Solomon and the Queen of Sheba has fascinated hearts for generations. In Scripture, their meeting is described with brevity and power—Solomon's wisdom, Sheba's awe, and the glory of God magnified in their encounter.

The Bible itself does not record an intimate relationship between Solomon and the Queen of Sheba, nor does it mention a child born to them. Those details come to us through other writings and traditions, most notably the **Ethiopian Kebra Nagast**, an ancient text that tells of their son Menelik, who is said to have carried the Ark of the Covenant to Ethiopia. Over time, this legend has become deeply rooted in Ethiopian history and culture.

In fact, within **Ethiopian Christianity and national identity**, this tradition is considered central and treated as historical truth. Even to this day, a chapel in Axum is guarded by monks who claim it houses the Ark of the Covenant itself—said to have been brought there by Menelik. Whether riddle, legend, or reality, it remains one of the most enduring mysteries of faith and history.

This novel, therefore, is a work of fiction. I have taken creative liberty in weaving romance and personal detail into the Biblical account, while striving always to honor the truth of God's Word. My aim is not to alter Scripture, but to bring its timeless truths into vivid life.

I believe these men and women of the Bible were not only figures of faith, but human beings with longings, struggles, strengths, and flaws. My hope is that this retelling helps you see them with fresh eyes and a deeper appreciation for the ways God works through both wisdom and love.

May this story stir both your imagination and your faith, pointing you back to the One greater than Solomon.

With gratitude and respect,

Rena Jones

Psst...Before You Go

If you enjoyed *Solomon and the Queen of Sheba*, would you take a moment to leave a review? Your thoughts mean more than you know—they help other readers discover these stories and encourage me to keep writing them.

Every single review is like a little spark that carries this series forward. Whether it's a few words or a paragraph, your voice makes a difference.

And if you haven't yet read *The Garden*, the first book in the *Great Romances of the Bible* series, I'd love for you to experience that story too. Both books were written with deep respect for Scripture and a storyteller's heart, imagining the love and humanity behind the timeless Word of God.

Thank you for walking this journey with me. Until the next great romance...

With gratitude,

Rena Jones

Made in the USA
Middletown, DE
18 January 2026

27261510R00106